"Wanna Know What I'm Thinking Right Now?" Tom Asked Susan Lee.

"No."

"I'm gonna get you, Susan Lee McCrae."

"No."

"Yep. And since you finally gave me a decent kiss, I'll—"

"That was *decent?*"

"Yeah."

"I hesitate to ask what you think is inflammatory."

He confessed, "I don't know. You haven't kissed me thataway...yet."

She gasped. "What did you think *that* one was?"

"I've forgotten. You mean like this?"

And darned if he didn't do the very same thing all over again.

Dear Reader,

Every month we try to bring you something exciting in Silhouette Desire, and this month is no exception.

First, there's the *Man of the Month* by Jennifer Greene, which *also* is the start of a charming new miniseries by this award-winning writer. The book is *Bewitched* and the series is called JOCK'S BOYS after the delightful, meddlesome ghost of an old sea pirate.

Next, Jackie Merritt's sinfully sexy series about the Saxon Brothers continues with *Mystery Lady*. Here, brother Rush Saxon meets his match in alluring ice princess Valentine LeClaire.

Lass Small hasn't run out of Brown siblings yet! In *I'm Gonna Get You,* Tom Brown learns that you can't always get who you want when you want her....

Suzanne Simms has always been asked by her friends, "Why don't you write some funny books?" So, Suzanne decided to try and *The Brainy Beauty*—the first book in her HAZARDS, INC. series—is the fun-filled result.

And so you don't think that miniseries books are the only thing we do, look for *Rafferty's Angel* by up-and-coming writer Caroline Cross. And don't miss Donna Carlisle's *Stealing Savannah,* about a suave ex-jewel thief and the woman who's out to get him.

Sincerely,

Lucia Macro
Senior Editor

Please address questions and book requests to:
Reader Service
U.S.: P.O. Box 1325, Buffalo, NY 14269
Canadian: P.O. Box 1050, Niagara Falls, Ont. L2E 7G7

LASS SMALL
I'M GONNA GET YOU

SILHOUETTE *Desire*®
Published by Silhouette Books
America's Publisher of Contemporary Romance

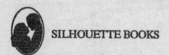 SILHOUETTE BOOKS

ISBN 0-373-05848-9

I'M GONNA GET YOU

Copyright © 1994 by Lass Small

Books by Lass Small

LASS SMALL

finds living on this planet at this time a fascinating experience. People are amazing. She thinks that to be a teller of tales of people, places and things is absolutely marvelous.

To all the striving people
who are determined to read
and to those who help them.
Salute!

One

Tom Brown was a photographer. He'd always been fascinated by perspective, lights and shadows. In the initial years, he'd been a real nuisance with surprise pictures of his multitudinous siblings up in Temple, Ohio.

His father Salty had told him, "Don't you ever take any pictures that would embarrass anybody. Do you understand me?"

When Salty Brown said that last sentence, the recipient *knew* the threat. So no one else ever saw Tom's file of those prints. He'd reluctantly burned the recognizable ones.

Tom was about twelve when Salty showed him a corner of the basement. He'd said, "This might be a good place for a darkroom to develop the negatives."

Tom helped put the darkroom together. So did the other siblings, male and female. Everybody living in the Brown household learned to clean, to take care of cars, to do repairs and become familiar with tools of most kinds.

Although Tom hadn't lived in Ohio for eight years, the darkroom was still there. In the years he'd used it, he'd showed his real and acquired siblings how to do the same things he'd learned. Since that time, the methods of developing and enlarging prints had advanced considerably.

Tom had been the class cameraman all through high school, and he'd sold prints to support his expenses. It was with some pride that he'd put himself through the school of fine arts at the University of Texas. Quite naturally, he'd majored in photography. Since his graduation, he'd made his living with his camera. His home base was Austin, TEXAS.

By now, it had been three years since his brother Bob had married Jo Malone on Christmas Eve at the family place in Ohio. When Bob and Jo had chosen to spend their honeymoon in their parents' attic, Tom had slyly contributed two purple condoms. But not quite trusting the amused Tom, their brother Cray had substituted some safer, utilitarian ones.

Bob and Jo still lived in the attic, and their second kid was on the way.

There could well be an attic fetish in the Brown genes, because Tom's brother Cray had lived in an attic in San Antonio for some time. Cray and Susanne had finally given up that Texas attic and moved into a little house in their neighborhood when they had their first baby.

Having lived in Texas for eight years, Tom had become an automatic Texas native and was well entrenched. He had an ear for the rhythm of the speech and he loved the Texans' strange use of words. A cyclone was "kind of breezy." Just like the U.S. government's decision to arbitrarily change the accurate labeling of The War Between the States to The Civil War, the National Weather Service insisted on calling cyclones... tornadoes.

Then there was Tom's appreciation of drama, and being a child of the actress Felicia, that came quite naturally. The underplaying of drama is so exquisitely done by Texans.

For the past two years, Tom's camera interest had been in the middle of a stark period. He found West Texas lent itself quite well to his need for the simplicity and drama of that land. There were no rentable places in the sparsely populated area.

His quasi-brother, Tweed, said, "Come live with us."

Tom had drawled, "Well, I can surely agree Connie is superior, but do you really think she'd be willing for me to share you all's bed?"

Tweed had laughed.

It was Tweed's boss, Sam Fuller, who found a place for Tom with the Petersons. There Tom had settled in and become a part of the Peterson routine.

One day Tom was out and about, through the deserted countryside, which was filled with cedar trees and the relentless mesquite. He was filming sparse images with his exceptional camera, watching, seeing and appreciating. And he saw the dog.

The animal was at the top of a slight natural fold, which came down along the rise. It showed the animal usage that followed a water run when it rained. It was impressive in that area that the dog was in full view.

Like wild creatures, the dog hadn't learned to stay out of sight and not call attention to itself.

The dog didn't look like a wild one, even though it was tacky and careful. It had a sense of place that a wild animal wouldn't have flaunted, nor was it as careful. It was a yellow shorthaired animal and quite large, with a thick neck and short ears. It was kind of worn looking. Along its side, its ribs showed through the dirty yellow coat. There was no collar.

While Tom had a rifle in his car, he never carried a gun. He was opposed to violence. He touched his belt knife. He didn't want to be in a fight with that big a dog, having only a knife. Since Tom was some reckless distance from his car, he considered the dog.

The dog watched him.

Tom wondered how it had gotten there? An unknown survivor of a car wreck? Maybe somebody died in a crash, and when people found the car and the dead driver, they hadn't realized a dog had been along? In spite of the undulating terrain, people tended to drive fast out in that sparse land, which was equally sparse of humans and of humans' vehicles.

Tom said in a calming way, "What you doing out here, boy?"

The dog sat down, but he was not relaxed. While he looked around, his attention was on Tom.

"I've got something to eat and some water in the car. Come along." Then he added with some edgy humor, "But not *too* close."

Tom turned away and kept to a careful walk. If the dog was a predator, he didn't want to stimulate any interest in a chase. He glanced back as casually as he could, and he saw that the dog watched him. But it didn't follow.

"Come on, boy, I've got water."

About the third time Tom repeated that, and on impulse, he added, "Heel."

Then, curious, he waited.

The dog stood up and looked back; then he came slowly down toward Tom. Tom was aware of some activity in his nervous system and felt the fine hair along his spine rise while his muscles tensed.

He wasn't afraid. Browns think they can handle anything, because Salty taught them so much. But Tom was ready.

While the dog followed enough, he didn't actually heel. He looked around, as any male does in any circumstance.

Somebody had lost a good dog.

At an awkward place for the dog to clean, there was a dried tar-blood-coated area on the back of his neck. His alertness was dull. He didn't beg or try to be friends. But he did go along after Tom in a disinterested manner, as if there were no other place to go.

Tom took off a hubcap and rinsed it before he poured water into it. The dog was sitting a distance away and watched. He rose with the first pouring of water but stopped as the rinsing water was thrown away.

Tom held out the refilled hubcap and coaxed, "Here, boy."

The dog didn't move. It became restless and edgy, its pink-gray tongue slid around its mouth, but the dog backed away.

Was the dog a runaway? Had someone been harsh as he'd tried to catch the dog?

Tom advanced slowly, talking soothingly. He set the hubcap about a third of the way between him and the dog. Then Tom backed up slowly, not talking.

The dog whined and was restless. It wasn't sure.

Tom returned to his car and eased the door closed.

The dog approached the hubcap pan and quickly lapped up the water, then tore itself away and ran a distance before it stopped and looked back.

Slowly Tom got out of the car, took some of his sandwiches and the jug of water back to the hubcap pan and filled it again. Then he laid the sandwiches beside the pan and returned to his car.

With its thirst relieved, the dog could wait. He sat down and watched.

After a time, Tom got out of the car and piled a marker of stones supporting a dead branch of a thorny mesquite tree with his handkerchief tied to one branch.

Back in his car, he started the motor, and the dog watched him drive away.

That evening at supper, Tom told the tolerant Petersons about the dog. His hostess, Mim Peterson, was a calm, gentle, pregnant thirty-nine-year-old who already had five stair-step kids. As she always was—about any breathing thing—Mim was concerned about a wild dog and glanced down the supper table at her husband.

Tom had commercially sold eighty-some-odd pictures of the rugged, forty-year-old Geo Peterson, who didn't hold still for it at all. And he accepted his model's fee, not believing it was his due. Even at the table without his Stetson, Geo was the perfect rugged man.

Geo said, "I've heard of a dog like that being around. Must be a wanderer."

Tom countered, "He knew the word 'heel.' While he didn't actually heel, he did follow me."

Geo took an impatient breath and asked his wife in disgust, "You know what's gonna happen?"

She nodded. "He'll bring it here."

Distastefully, Geo asked, "We got room for another dog?"

She smiled but didn't reply. The kids grinned, sharing the knowledge of what was sure to come.

Geo shifted in his chair in a very disgruntled way and told Tom, "You're a nuisance. You have to know that."

They all laughed. Geo not only said that same thing about Tom taking his picture, but he said it about anything he had to get done that he didn't want to do. He didn't want to go out and find some dumb dog that had gotten itself lost. Obviously Geo had had to do something like that too many times before.

Annoyed, Geo moved in his chair and shifted his booted feet. He frowned and cast irritated glances at Tom and down the table at his own smiling wife. He said to Tom, "You set him some food?"

"Yep."

"Then he can wait until tomorrow."

Tom beamed, the kids laughed and Mim got up and went to the other end of the table to give Geo a kiss.

He grumbled, "The things a man has to do to get kissed would shock a normal person."

So the kids all said they'd go along and help with catching the dog, and then they laughed through the kisses Mim gave them.

When Mim came to Tom, Geo held up his hand like a traffic cop and said, "I get the one for him."

In spite of Tom's protests, Mim sat her pregnant bulk on Geo's lap and kissed him again. He held her there, keeping her on his lap. He shifted his fork to use his left hand to eat the rest of his meal. He occasionally fed Mim a little, lifting the fork to her mouth, opening his as hers opened and closing his as hers closed.

Tom found watching that was erotic.

The kids accepted the parents' conduct with only amused smiles and not much attention. It was obvious their parents were always affectionate.

Tom observed their actions with envy, and he thought it was no wonder they were going to have their sixth kid.

When dinner was over, the pair was still sitting that way. Tom helped clear the table and stack the dishes in the dishwasher. He didn't have to, but Mim was sure pregnant, and he felt the need to help her.

Tom went out onto the porch that was across the entire front of the big, old house, and he found the rocking chair he'd bought and added as his own to those already on the porch.

He sat in the cool of the evening and looked out over the land. He wasn't contented. He envied the Petersons for what they had assembled and the way they felt about each other. He was a little jealous of their ease with the feelings they shared, the way they communicated and their tolerance and enjoyment of their lives.

So circumstances had seen to it that Tom was already ripe to really look at a woman.

As Tom looked around from the Petersons' porch, he thought theirs was a good place. Very few actual Texans called their land a ranch. No matter the size, they referred to the land as their place. The Peterson place was a very pleasant harbor for Tom. He was accepted by the family with the casualness that his parents gave at their own house—up in the northeast part of Ohio.

Tom automatically cleaned his own room, changed his own sheets and did his own laundry. He had free run of the Petersons' place, and he was allowed to tag along with Geo and take pictures, just as long as he didn't get in the way and there were no camera flashes. That challenged Tom's remarkable camera to do a superb job.

Tom spent almost half of his time in the allotted corner of the shed, where there was a faucet for water. There, he and Geo had contrived a darkroom.

The Petersons all exclaimed over the pictures Tom made of them and of their place. Tom gave copies of those to the family, and most were framed and hung all through the house along with the usual oils of blue-bonnets. It would be un-TEXAN not to have at least one painting of bluebonnets.

He had a wonderful picture of the very pregnant Mim hanging clothes on the line in a brisk breeze. The patterns of the windblown garments, the lights and shadows made a wonderful composition. There were wind-ruffled chickens around her feet, and the littlest Peterson was pulling on Mim's skirt, making her baby belly really obvious.

When Mim saw the finished picture she laughed and swatted Tom on his shoulder, but she asked for a copy to put into the baby book of the new-to-be little Peterson.

* * *

Tom almost didn't get back to the dog the next day. Geo had to go out to help another rancher who had a broken fence and stock had gotten loose.

That kind of thing came first. So Geo and the hands all left with the exception of Willy, who kept the milk cows and pets in hand and the kids from killing themselves trying to ride the goat.

That's why it was Tom who drove Mim to the area hospital when she went into labor. For years, the Petersons had had a two-way radio for Mim's communication, so they called Geo to meet them there.

Everything was fine until they had to take Mim into the delivery room, and it was then that Geo fainted. That big rock of a man!

Tom was alarmed, but everybody else laughed and chuffed. Geo always fainted—every single time.

And that was when Tom saw her.

He simply stared as she hustled around getting the smelling salts and helping. She was wearing a volunteer aide's uniform. And she never gave him a glance—as he stared, mesmerized.

No woman, any age, had ever been that unaware of Tom, and her total unawareness was somewhat surprising. He studied her and found she was perfect. Slender, her body was a delight of curves. Her honey blond hair was in a knot at the back of her head, and her head was circled by a cloth band, tidily holding her hair away from her face. When she smiled, she had a little dimple at the right corner of her mouth. None of her smiles had been for Tom.

What was her name?

He couldn't see the color of her eyes because she didn't even glance at him.

So with Mim in the delivery room and Geo out cold on the floor, Tom was concentrated on a woman. He waited for her to glance up at him so that he could smile. He knew he had a killer smile.

She glanced up at him, and without turning a hair looked on beyond him! Then she went back to reviving Geo.

Never before had Tom ever seen a woman who could look at him and look on past him without any hesitation or recognition of him as a man. He felt a little indignant.

His features were regular. His eyes were blue, his hair was thick and black and tended to curl. His body was like Salty's as a young, fit man. He was taller than Salty. When that had happened, it had been something that pleased Tom in a way that—even then and with some humor—he had recognized his pride in being taller than Salty as being rather asinine.

Just the fact that Tom recognized the asininity showed his humor.

Tom knew he moved well in boots. He had studied and copied the casual slouch that was TEXAN to the core. It made a man look as if he could uncoil into something very dangerous. He'd never been tested as yet. But he'd watched Tweed and Geo, and Tom knew how to go about doing something similar if it was ever necessary. If Geo could move like that at forty, it was only logical Tom could do it even better at twenty-six. Maybe.

Geo began to come out of his faint. He was pale, but it was impossible for any of them to consider him fragile. He was such a hunk that his fainting only endeared him to everyone. He could be vulnerable. He loved his wife. He melted all their hearts.

In a shaky voice, Geo asked, "Is it over?"

Ignoring the staff, Tom replied, "Not yet."

Geo groaned and flapped a hand at the smelling salts. "Get that stuff away and let me go out again."

They all just chuckled and scolded him.

Geo held his head and shook it slowly. "I'm going to get that vasectomy."

The witnesses hooted.

"No. I really am. I can't go through this again."

One of the aides exclaimed, "*You* can't!"

And Geo replied, "No. Mim just has to give up having kids."

Tom mentioned, "She doesn't get that way all by herself."

Eyes closed, lips pale, Geo groaned, "She's careless."

That Miss Priss, who wouldn't look at Tom, sassed, "*She* is!"

Through white lips, with his eyes still closed, Geo agreed. "She's so tempting, and she does that deliberately."

Miss Priss said, "How like a man to blame a woman."

Tom thought, Oh, hell, she's one of those women! He put in his oar. "My mother had twenty-eight kids."

He'd finally gotten her to look at him fully. She had green eyes and she was horrified! "No!"

"Yep." He would do about anything to keep her looking at him, so he added, "And she has a career on the stage."

"How?" the aide gasped.

Tom had the audacity to explain kindly, "Organization."

She gave him a look that was completely unbelieving and—

Dr. Sanford came through the door with a little wiggly baby and a big smile, as he said, "A boy!"

Predictably, Geo protested, "But you promised us another girl!" He rolled to his feet and reached for the baby.

The doctor explained, "He changed his mind."

Geo took the baby into his hands and looked at him, as he said, "But we only have one girl! She'll be spoiled rotten. We needed another girl!"

Sanford reminded Geo, "Mim's had six kids."

"I know. I *know,* but we can't just have one girl in that raft of males. She'll be ruined with all the attention."

"Adopt some." That was Miss Priss's suggestion.

"I want her to look like Mim." Geo was stubborn.

Grinning, Tom said, "Congratulations."

"Thanks, Tom. We'll name this one for you. How about being his godfather?"

"Why..." Tom was so pleased! "Why, I'd be honored."

Geo kissed his new son's forehead and said to the baby, "We'll keep you." Then he handed the baby to Tom and said, "I've got to see to Mim."

So Tom was holding the baby, whose blanket was slipping, and darned if the kid didn't squirt at that very minute! Tom ducked his head away and scolded, "Here, here, you rascal! That's a-way out of line. You're not supposed to do that to your godfather!"

And Miss Priss laughed. She had a lovely laugh. But she was laughing *at* him. She was a little smug because Tom had been squirted by his new godson. Tom knew

right away that she needed some man's controlling
hand on her. He'd volunteer.

Another aide pulled little Tommy's blanket over him
in protection.

But Miss Priss did bring a cloth and efficiently wiped
Tom's face. She hadn't intended doing it. She tried to
give him the cloth, but both his big hands were suddenly very occupied with holding the baby, and Tom
was clever enough to pretend holding a kid was new to
him. So she cleaned Tom's face.

It was wonderful.

She finished briskly and started to turn away. Tom
said, "Along my nose."

She wiped there.

He said in a gruff voice, "By my left eye." He closed
that in a wink.

She wiped that area.

He suggested, "Under my chin." And he lifted his
face, but he watched her through his narrowed eyes.

She hesitated.

She wasn't dumb. She suspected he was prolonging
her attention to him. He smiled.

She gave him a snooty glance of impatience and left
him there.

Tom looked down at the miracle in his hands. How
amazing. He remembered the first puppy he'd held. He
became mushy. He said softly, "Hello, Thomas Peterson."

The kid squinched up his face, and his lower lip
trembled as he moved and squirmed.

Tom's male voice was gentle, "You have such an interesting time ahead of you. You will see so many
wonderful things and learn things you never believed
possible."

The kid yawned.

Tom smiled at his godchild. Then with practiced skill, he held the baby along his left forearm, cradling the baby's head in his big hand as his other hand rearranged the blanket around the tiny kid. As he was lifting the new, little Tommy easily up to his shoulder, Tom glanced up. There she was, Miss Priss, standing in the doorway and silently still. She was watching him.

Tom froze.

She regarded him for a longer minute; then she came briskly into the room and said, "I'll take him to the nursery."

"I can carry him. He's comfortable. Just lead us along. I'm his godfather, and he feels safe with me."

"I can't fathom why."

"Do I look—inept?"

She glanced up, but she said nothing. She led him to the nursery down the hall.

When they got there, Tom was surprised to find himself reluctant to let go of the baby. All those people there were strangers. He said to Miss Priss, "What's your name?"

She hesitated.

He said, "I have to have a name so I can find out if you all are treating my godson with the proper care."

She lifted her chin. "Miss Holsome is in charge of the nursery."

"Where do you work?"

"I'm a volunteer."

"Where?"

She tilted her head a little. "Wherever they need me."

"You wipe a face pretty good."

"I'll see to it that's on my report."

He allowed his eyelids to close a little. "If they'd ever want a full report, I could examine you for them. I wouldn't mind the nuisance of that."

"How kind."

"My name's Tom Brown."

"Yeah. Sure."

"It really is. My daddy's name is Salty, he was a sailor, and my mother's name is Felicia."

"She's the actress?"

"All the time." He nodded with his words. "She's magnificent."

"You have a mother complex?"

"I have an admiration of skill."

She considered him with her head tilted back in a rather arrogant manner. She asked, "Are *you* skilled?"

"I'm working on it." And a smile crept out unbidden.

"In what?"

"Getting a snippy woman to let down her shield. I'm harmless."

She snorted.

She did! A lady like her snorted! He couldn't believe it, and he laughed. "Now what would make a lady like you so disbelieving of a good man?"

"Who says you're a good man?"

"Ask Mim."

She looked uncertain. Then she asked, "How long's she known you?"

"Over a month."

"A *month!*"

"Yeah. That's a lifetime on a place like theirs."

"From what I understand, you're in the shed most of the time."

He tilted his head back just a little and his eyes closed a bit. So she'd asked around about him? "I'm not being disciplined," he explained with a tad too much seriousness. "I have a darkroom in there. I'm a photographer. It just so happens I have a camera along with me?" That was a questioning do-you-understand statement. "Would you be so kind as to hold little Tommy—now don't wake him up—so's I can begin to chronicle his days?"

"Well, I could. But you could put him..." She looked around. The hall had no tables or chairs. "I could hold him. But you really ought to have his mother or father."

"I think it's important for any male to be seen early with a beautiful woman who isn't kin. It gives him confidence."

Tom didn't let go of the baby. Being smart, he carried the kid with him to his jacket and to the small, innocent-looking camera nesting in the pocket, waiting to intrude into Miss Priss's life.

Tom took pictures. He even took some of his godson. When he'd just about exhausted his film supply, he stopped and said, "I do need some of the parents."

She nodded. "They're waiting for the baby in the—"

"Tommy," Tom supplied. "Thomas Peterson."

"They're waiting for Tommy Peterson in the nursery."

"I have to kiss him first. I have to give him the godfather kiss."

She was surprised and looked down at the baby, then back up at Tom. "Godfather?"

"Yeah. I'm responsible for him now. If his parents louse up, I have to see to it that he's raised right."

That appeared to surprise her. "You?"

"Yeah. Don't you think I can?"

"You don't look the type."

So of course he asked, "What type do I look?"

She was serious. "Dangerous."

"Not to a kid like Tommy."

Watching him with the baby, she considered that. "Perhaps not."

"Then how could I be dangerous?"

She didn't reply.

He waited. But she was silent. So he leaned over, and his cheek touched her breast as he kissed the baby's forehead. To do that exactly, he'd had to put his hand to Miss Priss's back and hold her still.

He slowly raised his head from the baby, who lay in her arms. Tom looked into her face. Her eyes were serious. He said in a husky voice, "How could I be dangerous to anyone?"

And she replied readily, "To women."

Two

After seeing to it that neither Mim nor Geo needed anything from him, Tom went out and drove to the site where the dog had been. It was a good thing Tom had put up the marker or he'd never have found the place.

The hubcap was dry, the sandwiches were gone, there had been all sorts of intrusive creatures around the area. It was fascinating that many variations of prints could be made in twenty-four hours in such a seemingly deserted place. He didn't know the identity of most of the tracks. There were different creatures in TEXAS. Mice were obvious. A cougar? Now that was sobering. None of the tracks was human.

Of course there were still his own boot marks, and it was interesting to Tom to note that the dog's footprints were over boot imprints. Tom saw where the dog stopped and sniffed at his scent on his boot marks...and the cougar had tested for the scents of all the marks in the area. Everything there was edible to the cougar... including Tom Brown.

Tom went back to the car and got his rifle.

Tom tracked around as he'd been taught by his father long ago, and recently by Geo. Tom saw the entrance, investigating prints and exit of the cougar in that area. There was no sign that the dog had been set upon. It was such a big dog that perhaps the cougar had chosen not to confront him?

Tom's camera took remarkable shots of the paw prints and the crossing of the cougar's over his own boot prints. It would make a catching light and shadow print. He'd call it: "Pursuit." With that title, the size of the paw on the boot print was a whole story.

Tom thoughtfully replenished the water and food. Then he went to the Petersons' place and found the kids all exuberant over little Tommy's reality. Tom understood that Geo and Mim had called the kids.

The oldest of the Peterson joint endeavor was fourteen. Even he was smiling and shaking his head. "We had asked for another girl."

"May we go with you back to the hospital? Mom and Dad said it would be okay. We want to see Tommy. Check him out and see if we want him around."

Tom reared up to his full height and said with exaggerated indignation, "He's my godson!"

And the eldest retorted, "Since Dad called, and told us that, we've talked. With you as godfather, we need to look this kid over and see if he measures up."

Tom had to laugh. Then he said smugly, "You'll see."

The fourteen-year-old replied, "We figure there're more of us than you and we can control the blight of your influence."

Blight of influence? Mim was teaching the kids English? She needed to work on their respect for their elders.

With that passel of kids rooting around among the photographic paraphernalia in his car, Tom drove them to the hospital that late afternoon. Tom figured to dump the kids on Geo and take Miss Priss home.

He showed up looking a bit scruffy from his resupplying the dog and his camera's distraction to footprints in the dusty soil. Such concentration was detrimental to schedules.

He asked one orderly, "When do the volunteer shifts change?"

"In about fifteen minutes."

Tom smiled. He didn't ask her name because in that consolidated hospital, out in the middle of nowhere, gossip was probably even worse than in a regular hospital.

Carefully, before time to change shifts, Tom was at the middle of the lower hall to catch Miss Priss before she could exit either front or back. The registration desk was there. People's comings and goings could be monitored by those at the desk.

At that time, in that area, security was not yet needed. The only visible personnel besides those at the desk were those at the back exit, at the emergency entrance.

Miss Priss came down the hall, talking to another woman who was about her age. Tom hoped Miss Priss was at least eighteen. He thought she must be because she was so snippy. And he knew that she recognized him as an intact male who had all his parts and most of the instincts. He wouldn't readily kill a man. She would already recognize his obvious restraint. He was a talker. She had to know that already.

He straightened from his stance against one corner of the cross halls and took the toothpick from his mouth to slide it into his shirt pocket. He was couth. He sauntered over, as he'd practiced, mimicking his big foster brother Rod's male prod.

Blocking their way, Tom smiled at the other young woman as he took Miss Priss's elbow. Then he looked at her from under the Stetson, and his eyes glittered.

She saw them do that, and her lips parted while her eyes got larger.

He said to the other woman, "Excuse us, will you?"

The other grinned at Miss Priss and said, "See you Thursday."

Tom caught that. Today was Tuesday. She wasn't there again until Thursday. It was a good thing to know. He could have spent the whole next day looking for that unfriendly woman.

As if relating rote, Miss Priss said, "Tommy is fine. So are his parents. Geo hasn't fainted again." Her snippiness included a humorous glint in her eyes.

He said, "I'm here to take you home."

"I have a ride."

"Tell them you have other plans." His voice was smoky.

"I don't break dates."

He exaggerated his real shock. "You're old enough to date?"

"You like juveniles?"

"Get 'em young and raise 'em right."

"Good gravy." She lifted her head back as she pulled the corners of her mouth down in a wonderful display of tolerant censure.

He smiled. "I'll take you . . . home."

"Thanks, anyway." She lifted her elbow from his gentle grip, turned her back on him and started down the hall to the front entrance.

He sauntered along, watching her fascinating body react to her quick steps, and he got there in time to open the door for her—by hurrying enough and stepping first on the automatic opener. He bowed and swept off his Stetson.

She passed him by, but he saw that she was controlling her amusement. Making a woman feel amused was a good toehold.

Outside, Tom looked around from under the brim of his resettled Stetson. Seeing a man leaning against a red car down the line, he asked, "Where's your ride? My car's right over there." Closer.

She said, "By the red car."

She didn't walk on past him. So he asked, "Red car? Which one?" Then he counted the red cars. "There's two, three, four-five-six, seven-eight-nine—"

She said patiently, "He's standing by it, right over there."

She had pointed with her chin, but Tom didn't immediately look at the distasteful, lecherous, unsuitable male who didn't even stir from the side of his car. He asked, "You serious about somebody that won't even come to the door for you?"

"Not yet."

"Good." Then Tom stared down the line of cars and surveyed the male body alongside the red car. He looked like a perfectly nice person. Good body. His own stare was serious at seeing some other man being with Miss Priss. He was probably older than she by ten years. He was probably established and ready to take on a wife and care for her. Tom observed, "He looks like a woman beater. Your daddy check him out?"

"I've known him for a long time. He went with my cousin."

He calculated soberly, "She get too old for him?"

"She married another man."

"Oh." Tom assimilated that. "And he dates you as a substitute for your cousin?"

"They were just good friends and always in crowds."

"That you know."

"She's my cousin. I know. I was along most of the time with some of the other people."

"She was smart to escape him. He looks mean."

Miss Priss laughed. "You should write."

"I take pictures. I have some of you."

She was appalled. "By the pond?"

His ears perked up. "What goes on at the pond?"

"Then if you ask that, you don't know? You weren't there?"

He urged wickedly, "What goes on at the pond?"

"None of your business."

"Nude swimming," he guessed.

"You're guessing."

"Sex? Wild and rampant sex!"

She sputtered, "No!"

"Shucks."

She took a slow step or two around him and on her way to the other man, the one by the red car.

"How does a man around here afford a car like that? He's probably selfish and stingy."

"No, no, no." She was amused as she shook her head. Watching the walk, she took another several steps in the direction of the man.

Using that smoky voice, he asked, "How long is your date this evening? When will you be home again? Where do you live?"

"You're nosy."

"I never was before now."

And she laughed. It was a wonderful sound that went into Tom and squiggled around. It was a taunting laugh that made a man want to try for another from her.

He asked, "What's your name?"

She looked back over her shoulder and replied, "Pudd'n pie."

"No, that's mine. But I've never made any maiden cry."

"You're new around here. Do you stay long enough anywhere to know if you've left a woman crying?"

"If one had, I would have known."

She took another step and another, then, away from him.

He followed along, lagging so that she wouldn't move quickly toward the waiting man.

The man straightened. He'd been watching intently. He was controlling himself, but he was tense and alert.

Tom told her, "My name's Tom Brown. I'm from Ohio, but I went to TEXAS University and graduated from there. I'm a photographer. I'd like you to pose for me."

"Nude?"

"If you insist, but I'd—"

And she snorted again.

"How can such a lady like you snort thataway?"

"You're the only man I've ever done that with, because I don't believe you at all."

He was incredulous. "Why ever not?"

"You look dangerous."

"You've said that before. I'm putty. Tell me your name. I could go inside and find out, but then they would all know I'd asked, and their attention would be on you."

"You don't think it isn't already? Do you realize from the time you interrupted my walking with Billy Jean and now out here with all those who are glancing out of the windows that each one realizes you've been after me?"

"How'd you know that?"

"Billy Jean is—"

"No, not Billy Jean. How'd you know I'm after you? I only asked to take you home so's I could arrange for you to ride a horse so's I can take pictures of you. I pay model fees. Ask Geo. I irritate the hell out of him, but he is so photogenic that I can sell any picture of him I send out. I bet a nickel that I could sell those of you. You're a natural. This awkward waylaying encounter here is strictly business, and it had to be done thataway only because I don't know your name." He gave her his best unthreateningly serious look.

She blushed a little, and on her it was riveting. She sputtered, "I thought you were a lecher."

"Oh, I *am* one, but now and then I'm also very seriously committed to work. That's taking pictures, and I have to have models. Go ahead. Go back upstairs and ask Geo if I'm trustworthy with a camera. I'll tell what'shisname to run along, and I'll take you home when you come back down here."

She hesitated and gave him a level look. "I'll ask Thursday."

"I'll be here."

"You could charm a woman right out of her socks."

His voice low and intimate, he countered, "Not right away. She'd have to be willing. 'Course, I don't ever recall being triggered by bare feet." He allowed her that assurance.

She tilted her head back and gave him a sly sideways glance from under mostly closed lids. "And if she wasn't willing?"

He replied bracingly, "I'm a professional." She could take that to mean his photography.

He glanced down the cars and saw the man by the red one was not only very alert, he was then standing in front of his car, watching down the line to them.

Tom said kindly, "Since he's watching so scared and trembling and insecure, you don't have to kiss me goodbye."

Her lips parted in amused, indignant shock, and she took a quick breath. She couldn't think of any response right then.

He then matched her steps until they reached the waiting man. It was apparent that the man wasn't sure what Tom would do. He moved his head rather jerkily, trying to see them both and judge what he might have to do.

Tom said easily, "Howdy. I'm Tom Brown." And he had the gall to hold out a friendly hand for a shake.

Taken unaware, the man automatically grasped the offered hand and replied, "Garth Pippins."

"Ahh. I understand you're leaving the area. Will it be soon?"

Garth was surprised by that and looked at Miss Priss for guidance.

She moved her head up and allowed it to roll sideways in exasperation as she sighed. She asked Tom, "Did I ever say that?"

Tom was innocent. "You didn't tell me it was a secret!"

"He isn't!"

Tom was earnest. "Isn't . . . a secret?"

She was elaborately patient as she carefully enunciated, "He isn't leaving town."

Garth was literal. "Well, next fall I have to go to Fort Worth for about ten days."

Tom nodded in little bobs, as if that only confirmed what he'd asked. He said to Miss Priss, "See you Thursday." Then he added with a very telling look, "Behave yourself."

She retorted, "You are the most annoying individual I've *ever*—"

In commiseration, Tom agreed, "I know. You have to learn not to lure men to you."

So Garth was shocked. "You *lured* him?"

And she said, "N—"

"She's subtle." Tom was the peacemaker. "She ought to behave reasonably . . . now."

Garth didn't know what to think, and Miss Priss was so indignant that she couldn't think of anything strong enough for a lady to get away with saying it!

Tom patted her shoulder once and got away before she could physically attack him. He trotted off to his own car and got in.

He passed them twice on the road and dawdled enough that they had to pass him. He smiled every time and waved a cheerful hand. But he found out where she lived.

Then he drove to the center of the sparse area and found directions to the mayor of that carelessly flung-out place. He had a nice visit while the mayor reshoed a horse of his. Tom was fascinated and took some pictures of his work. The mayor was pleased and earnest about posing just so.

Tom had introduced himself as a part of Geo Peterson's household. Geo was well-known and respected, and that was Tom's identification.

He talked to the mayor about the beauty of TEXAS, photography and resettling around there. He asked whose house that was just before the junction. It was a good house. Would there be any chance of buying it?

It wasn't long before he found out the aide's last name was McCrea. He also learned that the McCreas could possibly sell . . . in a hundred years or so, but not before then.

Tom chuckled in appreciation for the wordage.

The next day, although it was quite a distance out of his way, Tom drove past her house twice. Having grown up hip deep in sisters, Tom knew any reasonably mature female in a house keeps one eye on the road to see who drives by. He wanted Miss McCrea to know he was interested.

He also went out and replenished the water and food for the dog. And he had more dramatic pictures of paw-bird-creature prints, crossing and passing and overlapping. For two days, now, he hadn't seen the dog again. What if the dog had left the area?

What if he had died?

On Thursday morning, carrying his cougar-rebuffing rifle and very alert to being alone out there with strange watchers, Tom searched for the dog. He whistled shrilly, and he used his fingers in his mouth to create an even louder and longer whistle.

He waited, listening, turning his head. There was no sound at all. He'd even silenced the birds.

Tom spent Thursday afternoon in the shed with
Kyle, one of Geo's boys, who was interested in photography. Tom developed the rolls of film he'd shot,
showing how that was done. He had some really spectacular prints. They were so exciting to Tom that he
was thrilled.

If it hadn't been for the dog, Tom would never have
looked for those prints betraying the passing of creatures along the stretch of soft, accepting ground. He
wasn't a hunter. Seeing the tracks proved there were all
sorts of creatures in what Tom had thought was a
completely deserted place used only by birds and occasionally cattle.

Being Geo's son, Kyle knew more of the tracks.
"This one's an armadillo. Those are a fox. That there's
a rattler."

Tom blinked. He was aware of snakes. No one can
live in Texas very long without being warned, "Never
step over a log or off a ledge without looking!" That
was basic advice and went with the other warnings,
"Always wear a hat and never walk or drive along on
dry riverbeds!"

In eight years down in Texas, Tom had rarely seen
snakes. With proof there were snakes where the dog
had been, Tom began to worry about the dog. Did it
know not to fool with a snake? What had caused that
dried tar-blood wound on the dog's back? Something
bigger than most animals.

With developing the film, Tom showed Kyle those
first pictures of the dog standing between the brush on
the rise at the top of that little fold in the land.

"We've heard there was a dog like this around and
about. You saw him! Nobody seems to see him or find

him. There've been chickens lost, and everybody thought it was the coyotes.''

Later that afternoon, Tom took flowers to Mim. And he said to her, "Which of the McCreas is the one who helped out Tuesday?"

"Susan Lee." Mim was holding her new baby; and she was only replying but not paying much attention.

Tom smiled. So her name was Susan Lee McCrea.

And that's what he said when she came along the hall to fetch little Tommy Peterson back to the nursery. Tom tilted his Stetson politely and said, "Well, hello there, Susan Lee McCrea."

"Who told?"

So Tom listed the two people he'd consulted, mentioning the mayor first.

"You know Johnny Boy?"

"Quite well."

"And Mim blabbed?"

"She was distracted by my godchild at the time and just went ahead and said your name without paying it any attention." He smiled down at the disgruntled Susan Lee, and then he told her in a soft, gruff voice, "I'm gonna git you."

She lifted her nose and said, "Oh, no. No, you're not, either."

"I'll be waiting for you at five to carry you home. And we can talk about how you can pose for me on a horse."

"I'm not a model."

"You're what I'd like to use as a model. I'll be out there in the parking lot, waiting. I'll take you safely home."

It wasn't long after that when one of the other aides came along. She saw Tom, and her eyes widened and her eyebrows went up. Then she smiled and blushed. She said, "I have a note for you."

"That's neighborly of you. Thank you. How come you had to write it?"

"It isn't my note. It's from Susan Lee McCrea."

"Oh, yes. I know her. Thank you kindly."

So he opened the sealed envelope and there was, indeed, a note. It read, *Don't wait around for me. Go on home. Susan Lee McCrea*

Tom looked at the message thoughtfully and considered what he should do. So he made his goodbyes to the Petersons, saying he wouldn't be there, at the house that night for dinner. Then he went down the stairs and out the front door.

Sure enough, next to his red car was Garth Pippins, standing there, waiting for Susan Lee McCrea.

Kindly, Tom went over to Garth and greeted him, sharing another handshake, then Tom said, "I have a note for you from Susan Lee?" He used the questioning statement that is peculiar to Texans, even those who are fairly new ones.

"A note? What for?"

"Yeah. I didn't read it. Want me to read it for you?"

"No. No. I can read it." So Garth opened out the paper and saw written, *Don't wait around for me. Go on home. Susan Lee McCrea.*

Garth looked up and said, "She's probably going to run pretty late. It was nice of you to bring down her note. Thanks."

Tom said, "Glad to oblige."

"Does she have a ride later, or should I come back?"

"I think one of the other aides has her car here. Susan Lee said not to bother about her."

"Well, I guess I might just as well leave then."

Tom soberly agreed, "Might as well."

"Tell her I'll call her tomorrow."

"If I should see her, I'll be sure to remember to do that."

"They've really been busy around here lately."

Tom shifted his feet so that he could sneak a glance at the entrance door. He didn't know how to hurry the man along. "Drive carefully."

"Yeah. Thanks again."

"Yeah." His reply didn't encourage any further conversation. He began to walk back toward the entrance, listening avidly for the sound of the Pippins' engine starting.

It finally did, and the car slowly backed and then began its slow way out of the parking lot. With a new automobile like that one, Pippins probably never drove over thirty miles per hour.

Tom hurried to the entrance to prevent any exit by Susan Lee and sure enough, just inside, he ran into that very person. He was surprised. "You leaving already?"

She was delayed because he blocked her way. She replied logically, "I generally leave at this time."

"I doubt that. There must be times when things get really hairy and all hands are needed."

"This is a very efficient hospital, and that sort of thing rarely includes the volunteers." She was kind in explaining.

Tom sought anything to keep her still for just a little longer. He asked, "Is there any other kid in the nursery that is handsomer than my godchild?"

"Beauty is in the eye of the beholder."

"What a quote! Is that one you made up?"

She laughed.

So he relaxed somewhat and said, "Would you go to dinner with me tonight? I was talking to the mayor about your house. Let's discuss your selling it to me."

"No."

"You don't want to sell?"

"No. It's not my house. I meant, no, I have another engagement."

"An *engagement!* Now that's serious. What sort of engagement is that?"

"I'm going to a barn dance with Garth."

"Oh." He looked thoughtful and bobbed his head a bit. Then, figuring enough time had passed for Garth to have snailed his way out of the parking lot, he said to Susan Lee, "I'll walk you out."

"How kind."

"Your momma must have been a southern lady. Your word choices and manners are a little different. Where was she brought up?"

He'd stopped and turned so that she, too, hesitated.

"Daddy was visiting a neighbor of hers over in South Carolina. Momma said he was the most intrusive and persistent man she'd ever seen."

Tom nodded in some more little bounces. "That explains it."

They were outside by then, and she looked around. Then she stretched and looked farther, but she couldn't see anyone standing, leaning against a red car, waiting for her. Garth wasn't there. "That's strange."

"What's strange?" Tom inquired with polite interest.

"Garth is always here."

Tom stretched up his added height and looked carefully around, taking quite a bit of time as he examined the entire parking lot. "By golly, you're right! He doesn't seem to be anywhere around. He's probably just been delayed a little. He'll turn up."

But Garth didn't show up. The pair stood and talked. She said to her escort, "You don't have to wait with me."

And he replied, "I enjoy being with you. It's a treat for me. As you know, the Petersons have an overload of males. And it's just real nice to talk to someone who sounds female. You're doing me a favor by letting me hear your voice."

So they talked, and he made her laugh. He told her about the dog and about teaching Kyle to develop film, and all the interesting tracks he'd found out there where the dog had been, and how he worried the dog was dead or had drifted off farther from that place.

She became interested. She watched his face, and he elaborated his search, and he just happened to have some of those developed pictures in his car. "Why don't I take you on to your house. Garth probably left a message there for you."

"Well . . ."

"It's already a quarter to six. If he was going to show up, he would have by now. He probably had a flat."

"I suppose."

"I'll just take you on home. And we'll see if they have a message about this."

"Are you sure you don't mind? After that note I sent you?"

"I'd be honored."

And he tucked her into his car.

Three

Tom drove Susan Lee along the roads, now known to him since he'd followed Garth along them and then practiced following them. He glanced aside to look at Susan Lee McCrea. She was really something for a man's eyes to rest on. She was so wonderful that it scared his stomach. Other organs reacted differently and with great stimulation.

The car windows were open in the evening sun. The wind pressed against her so casually. Her body was perfect. Well, she had all the parts any other woman had. Eyes, nose, mouth, neck, breasts—hers were perfect.

He found he had to mention, "You look good in my car."

She gave him the patient look one gives to a witless idiot who persists in mentioning silly things. She asked with some irony, "I have to be in your car to look good?"

"You'd look good in a battered tin tub on the river. I suppose I should have said that you make my car look good when you're in it."

She dismissed his compliment. "That's smooth talk."

"Is it? Well, hot dang! I hadn't known I could talk smooth."

"Hah."

"You sound disbelieving." His voice expressed some surprise.

"Any man whose tongue knows the right words, uses them. You are glib."

"I've never told that to another woman." He glanced from the road so that she could look into his honest eyes; then he looked back at the road. His face was serious.

She hesitated. She almost believed him. Then she shook her head in chiding. "A smooth talker can convince women he's never said such to any other woman."

And right on target, he gave her another of his honest glances and replied, "Then if you don't believe me, I must not be glib and that cancels your criticism of me. I'm not glib, therefore I spoke from my heart."

"A man like you has given his heart so many times, there's probably no part of it left."

"Give me your hand."

"You need help driving?"

His glance was the honest, serious one. "Give me your hand."

And she did! That she gave him her hand surprised them both.

He pressed her hand against his chest. Then he glanced again to her face, his eyes flicking tiny glances to see all of her. "Feel it?"

"What?"

He looked back at the road. "My thudding heart. It's pounding more than it should because you're sitting in my car with me and your hand is on my chest. I just hope it can survive the strain and excitement."

She chuckled in such amusement over him that she didn't really notice he'd changed their route.

He said, "You're making fun of me."

"I'm enjoying your sense of humor."

"What's humorous about my heart beating like a drum because I'm holding your hand to my chest. That's as erotic an experience as I've ever had!"

She burst out laughing.

"You sound disbelieving." He was earnest. "That's callous. You've heard men say something similar so many times that you don't believe it anymore. How many men have fainted because you touched their chests with your little hand?"

She was then aware of how big his hands were. His swallowed hers. She looked at his face, but he was watching the road. She said, "I'd prefer you to drive with both ha— Where are we going?"

"I want you to see the place where I saw the dog. Since you're a native around these here parts—how's that for local speech—I figure you know the area pretty well."

"I'm supposed to go to a barn dance."

"We'll be on time. I have the tickets."

"Now, Tom, how can I show up there with you instead of Garth?"

"Easy. I'll take you." He slid a quick, carefully logical glance at her.

"Has this sort of hustle worked for you before now?"

"I'm a novice. I was desperate, and you were no help at all. You just sashayed around and put your nose in the air and ignored me. If you hadn't just about smiled a time or two, I might have given up."

"You're about as tenacious as a bulldog!" Then she asked in a suspicious, narrow-eyed voice, "Did you run Garth off?"

"No."

"Did you say anything to him?"

"When?"

"Any time."

"I believe I told him my name and shook his hand a couple of days ago. He may well have realized, meeting me, that he hadn't a chance of a snowball in hell against me."

"You are modest."

"All us Browns are modest. You're not supposed to mention it because knowing we're modest embarrasses us."

"You are also dictatorial. I said I had to get on home. Just where are you taking me?"

He replied, "To see where the dog was."

"I haven't *time* for that."

"I have sandwiches and beer in the back seat, and I called your momma."

"When was that?"

He smiled at her very nicely. "Before I went out and gave your note to Garth."

"What note?"

"The one that said he was to go on home and not wait for you."

"What?"

Readily Tom repeated, "The one that said he was to go—"

"He! That was for *you!*"

"No! It was for *me?*"

"Yes! I wanted you to quit hanging around and bothering me."

"You bother me. I could hardly sleep last night."

"You are a lecher."

"No." He shook his head two slow times. "I'm a nice Ohio boy who is lonesome and needy. I need your company so I don't have to walk into that barn dance all by myself and stand around on the edge of everything, all alone and ignored."

"I can't imagine anyone having enough rudeness to manage to ignore you. Are you a traveling salesman?"

"No, I'm a top-notch photographer, and I worry about lost dogs and I try to think of some way to get your attention. I had to get you alone, away from all those other giggly aides and save you from that very literal and dull Garth."

"He's very sweet."

Tom was firm. "He'd be dull and ordinary."

"You're stimulating and different?"

"I'm what you've been looking for ever since you realized boys and girls are different for a good reason."

"And you're modest."

"Yes. I only accept fate, and my part in your life." He was watching along and somewhat distracted from his words. "It's right along here somewheres. Watch for my handkerchief tied to a mesquite branch propped up by rocks. By golly, I think I've already passed it. You are a distraction."

"I could go home."

"I can't risk you hitchhiking and getting tangled up with another unsuitable man."

"You could take me home."

"Well, I will! All in good time. Don't be so impatient. I gotta give the dog some water."

That, of course, stopped her. How could anyone, in that area, object to giving a stray creature water?

They drove back and forth along the sameness of that highway. They ate the sandwiches, and she had a soft drink. He had a beer.

He explained, "One is okay. I'm not influenced by consuming one beer. Two set me off. If I was to have two, then you'd have to be careful of your conduct, because two beers makes me friendly."

"I'll be careful."

"Well, you have been warned. Don't insist that I have the second beer unless you want to be surprised."

"I won't."

"You're much too biddable. You ought to stand on your own back feet and howl now and— There it is. Right there."

"What?"

"My handkerchief."

"Good gravy! You can see that!"

As he swung the car around and pulled off the highway, he mentioned, "Us Browns are sharp eyed. We see what we need to see every time."

"How did I get out here in this vacant landscape with you?"

He was surprised and explained, as to an afflicted mind, "You do know that both of the Petersons would—separately—skin me alive if I was to lay a finger on you? So you're safe for the time being."

"That's true."

"But I do have a car and a credit card, so I could skedaddle if'un you should tempt me too far. So it would be wise if you'd control your intense attraction to me for a while." He stopped the, by then, slowly moving car and turned to smile at her.

"That's the second time you've mentioned for a while. Just what do you mean by that?"

"Try to control your attraction to me."

She pulled in so much indignant air that she choked.

He lifted her arm up very high and his gaze was pleasured by that as he looked down her. He smiled and said, "I thought I told you not to do anything to catch my attention?"

She nodded and said with exquisite sarcasm, "Right. Sorry."

"Try harder."

"I will."

He got out of the car and opened the back car door to take out the rifle.

She became big eyed.

He saw that and explained very gently, "There's been a cougar's prints. Stay in the car. I'll fill the hubcap. I'd like to get it back for the car's sake of decency. It's embarrassed being without a hubcap, you understand, but I believe if I put out another pan, the dog might think I'm pulling something sly. He's spooked by people for some reason."

Then in a hushed voice Tom added, "Look. Right there between those scrubs at the top of the rise. He's *there!* I thought he might have moved on. This is the second time I've seen him. How about that."

And that's probably when he caught her emotional attention. She did look for the dog, but the switch of her attention from him to the dog did lag. She began to understand what sort of man he could be. He might already be that sort, and she would have to find out if it was so.

He said, "Can you shoot a rifle?"

Very quietly she replied, "Yes."

"Cover me, in case the cougar comes along inconveniently. I can't take the gun along if I intend to speak to that dog at all. Look. He hasn't left."

He slid the rifle along the back of the seat. "Careful. We don't want Dog to see that. He's spooked enough."

"Got it."

"The safety's on."

"Yes."

"I'm gonna try to get closer to him."

She whispered. "What if he attacks?"

"I've got my knife. Don't shoot unless he should get me down."

"Good grief."

"Sh-h-h. I'll be back."

He took the jug and some food scraps that were a mixture of meat and grains. He walked around the hood of the car, but then he was between her and the dog. He moved over to the right far enough so that she had a clear view of the dog.

She had to turn on the ignition key in order to roll down her window all the way. She moved to the middle of the console and was extremely stimulated and calm. She took the safety off the rifle and turned the ignition off.

The pan was empty and the food gone. Tom said, "Where you been, boy? Have you been eating and drinking here? Do you know all these others have been horning in on your food? You look better. I'll just fill this up. Come on down and have a drink. I'll back up a little. Come on, boy. There's water here for you and some good food. You ought to eat what you want before the others come along and feed here."

The dog did listen. Having been out in the brush for some time, the dog did know to look around and listen. He did that, but his attention always came back to the man.

Tom's voice was soothing and reassuring. Susan Lee thought it was alluring. She expected the dog to come immediately to Tom. If the dog had been a bitch, it would have. It did not.

It surprised Tom that the dog stood watching. He was more alert.

Tom squatted down, talking soothingly, coaxing the dog to come down. But, still, he did not.

Then Susan Lee saw Tom as he moved his arm very carefully in order to look at his watch. Time had passed. He had to get Susan Lee home so that she could change her clothing before they went to the barn dance.

Tom stood slowly, unthreateningly, and he told the dog what he was doing and why, just as if the dog could understand.

Tom walked slowly back to the car, looking back over his shoulder, and Susan Lee watched, tensely ready with the rifle.

Tom went to the car and got inside. He took the rifle from her hands and put the safety back on as he said, "You're a great backup. If ever I was in any danger, I'd want you backing me." He was serious.

So was she. "Thank you."

They watched the dog, who watched them back. Since he apparently wouldn't move until they left, Tom put the car into gear and slowly moved away. The dog stayed where he was.

Susan Lee said, "He'll eat the food."

"Yeah."

"You could put some sedative in his food now, since he trusts you."

Tom replied, "No. I have to let him make up his own mind. If I did sedate him, he would wake up panicked and fight us."

"You're probably right."

"It's what I'd do," Tom said. "If someone tricked me, I'd be mad as all bloody hell."

"You tricked me."

His eyes left the road and studied her for a fleeting second before he looked back at the road. "You were in danger of committing yourself to a dreary life. I didn't 'trick' you, I saved you."

She burst out laughing. "How could you alibi yourself out of something like that so smoothly and so convincingly?"

"By telling the truth."

"You tricked Garth," she reminded him.

Tom scoffed. "He doesn't count. Now, you know that I'd never fool you. I'll be honest and true to you."

She chided, "You're far too serious too soon."

"I want to start right with you."

So, of course, she asked, "Did you start 'wrong' with someone else?"

"How old are you?"

She accepted the shift in subject and replied readily, "Twenty-four."

In shock, he protested, "You're *that* old?"

"Yep." She grinned smugly.

His glance saw the smugness. "Shucks. I thought you were about sixteen, and I could get you young and raise you right."

"What is 'right' to you?"

He didn't even hesitate. "For you to be obedient, pliant, submissive and docile."

She put out one hand in a dismissive manner, adding a semishrug. "Sorry."

"Well, it might not be too late. We still might make it. It just depends on your attitude. We'll have to see. But it sure looks like this won't be nearly so easy as I'd thought." He sighed in a tired and put-upon way.

"I've never heard any man talk the way you do."

"That's Ohioan."

She drawled elaborately, "Honey, you talk Texan worse than most real Texans. It's how you apply the words in that slick and sassy way that surprises me. You don't even know me. For all you know, I might be a real witch."

His hand cupped his ear as he leaned his head a little sideways. He asked, "How's that? Say that word again."

"See? No other male I know would dare to be so mouthy. The word starts with a *W* and it means a woman who isn't very pliant."

He grinned. His voice was soft as butter on a hot day as he said, "You're here with me."

Did she grin and wiggle and agree? No. She said firmly and with some snip, "I was hijacked."

"You didn't struggle one whit."

Knowing he'd sneak a quick look at her, she had her eyes down and her mouth pinched as she tilted her head. She enunciated loftily, "What's a 'whit'?"

In a dangerous purr, he replied, "That's even less than a bit of a struggle . . . and you didn't."

"That's only because you're so smooth and crafty that I actually thought Garth would still show up. I had no idea you were so devious an— Where are we going?"

"We're closest to the Petersons', so I thought I'd change first and then we'd go on to your house so you can change. And you can call your momma and tell her you're on the way."

"So. She doesn't know I'm with you?"

"She probably thinks you're safely on some side road, necking with Garth."

"Are you implying that I'd be safe with Garth, all this time, making out on some lonesome road?"

His words were of marvelous surprise. "With Garth? 'Course you would."

"With you? Would I be safe with you?"

"We could find out." But as he looked at her he smiled just the tiniest little bit, and the lights danced in his eyes.

"I don't understand how you can be so wicked."

"It's you. I was never this way before in all my life."

"I don't believe you." She was prim.

They turned up the road to the Petersons' place, and the lane was as wild and woolly as all the rest of the countryside. No sign of civilization at all.

She looked around. "Is this their lane?"

"You spooked?"

"Well . . ."

"I've sworn that I'd behave if you did."

She was silent for a minute or so as she scanned the repetitious mesquites and the endless fence. "I'm not sure what I'm doing out here in the wilds of the countryside with you."

"We're getting acquainted, so's you'll become comfortable with me."

"Why would I want to do that?"

He was logical. "It makes it easier when we start having our kids."

She sighed impatiently.

"Don't fret. Petersons have indoor plumbing."

"Will anyone be there?"

He looked at his watch. "Probably."

"Probably!"

"Well, somebody has to be there to mind the place. I'm just not sure who." He frowned at her briefly. "You act like I'm carrying you off. I haven't even *started* on that phase of all this."

"What?"

He was patient and explained with great reasoning, "Like any battle plan, there are moves and shifts that have to be followed. Right? And—"

"What battle?"

"My storming the bastions to rescue you from Garth and the deadly life you'd live, if you had him to deal with all the time. It wouldn't be long before you'd have headaches instead of sex. And that's all it would be. No loving, slow and wonderful, just awkward coupling. And he'd be embarrassed—every time. The time will come, buttercup, when you'll realize that and look on me as your rescuer. Be sure you don't miss this opportunity to save yourself while I'm still here."

"I do not be-*lieve* this!"

"Do you really, actually, want a taste of *Garth?* I can't allow that. He'd ruin you and your impulsiveness. You'd stiffen your back and freeze by the time I got to you. You don't want that sort of experience. Stick around, and I'll prove it all to you."

"Do you realize we've just met?"

"You're a lucky woman."

She was silent. She studied the passing mesquite, the approaching two-track gravel road that ran away under the car and Tom's profile. She worked her mouth and took in quick, little breaths and started to speak any number of times.

Finally he said, "We're here."

And they were. It was a large house built close to the ground without a basement. The porch was across the front, with rocking chairs ready for comforting. The house was two-story and complicated. It could house not only their family but probably all the guests who wanted to stay there, too.

Tom drove up near the house, and there were all those kids around and dogs, cats, a goat, an old man who smoked a pipe that Susan Lee knew probably smelled really rotten. And there was Geo coming out the door.

It was sundown, for Pete's sake, and they were all interested in the arrival.

Saying "Hold still. I'll get the door," Tom got out of his side of the car and stretched. Then he waved to the interested mob as he walked around and opened her door. He needlessly took her elbow to help her out, and he called greetings and asked about Mim and the baby.

As the pair approached the porch, Mim came out. She said, "Well, hello, Susan Lee! Glad to see you."

And Susan Lee was surprised. "What are you doing home so soon!"

"I got lonesome there. And Tommy had to see where he'd be living."

Susan Lee laughed. She also relaxed. She greeted the kids, and she touched her nose with her knuckle every time she had to breath in while she met and spoke with Willy and his pipe.

Tom told Mim, "She might like to freshen up. We went out to replenish the dog's food and water. We saw him. He was there! He didn't come down, but he didn't run."

Geo said, "We could put something in the next batch of food."

Tom shook his head. "I'd rather not. I want him to come on his own."

Geo looked at his dogs. "What we need about now is a good-solid-wild-sorting-out, top-dog fight. You're a nuisance, Tom, do you realize that?"

"No. I'm a humanitarian."

"Wow." But Geo's tone was all wrong.

When Tom had had a quick rinse off and changed into clean clothing with a shirt and string tie, he found Susan Lee sitting on the porch, rocking, laughing at the outrageous stories the kids were telling. She was holding the new little Peterson, and to Tom's eyes she looked very natural doing that.

He asked, "Would you rather stay here or go to that stimulating barn dance?"

"I suppose I'd better go to the barn dance and explain—" She stopped and blushed.

"Did you call your momma?"

She nodded. She looked chidingly at Tom. "You'd called her."

"'Course."

He took Tommy from her arms with some care and held him away from his clean clothing. He told the new baby, "You behave, do you hear me? This is your stern and strict godfather speaking. Learn my voice. To hear it is to obey."

That set them all off.

Tom frowned at them and said, "I've got to start somewhere. This is logical. He's young enough, I might get a handle on him."

They hooted as he handed Tommy over to one of the other kids, already sitting in a rocker and demanding to hold the baby.

Mim said, "That'll get old fast. Just watch."

Susan Lee said, "Then call me."

But Mim replied, "I'd doubt you have the free time." And she caught Geo's glance and laughed.

As they got back into Tom's car in the wave of goodbyes and sly advice from Geo and the laughing Mim, Susan Lee asked Tom, "Why wouldn't I have any free time?"

Tom replied without any hesitation at all. "You'll be with me. I'll have to take you everywhere while you're hanging on my arm and around my neck, you'll be so taken with me."

She thought that was hilarious. She bubbled with laughter.

He smiled like a cat with a canary feather on his whiskers. "You got a good laugh, do you know that?"

"You're so funny."

"I haven't tapped funny as yet. I've been serious and truthful all this time."

That set her off into another peal of laughter.

They stopped off at the McCreas', and Tom sat on the porch with Susan Lee's father while she freshened up and changed. Her daddy was careful and asked any number of well-thought-out questions, to which Tom replied openly.

Mr. McCrea ended up saying, "That Geo Peterson is a sharp man who can read another man with a glance."

Tom agreed to that. "My brother, Tweed, works for Sam Fuller."

And Mr. McCrea nodded. He'd already found that out. By then, he might well have known more about Tom than Tom did.

The barn dance was fun. The women all wanted to dance with Tom, but he danced only with Susan Lee, keeping all the men from touching her. Quite seriously he explained to her, "I'm selfish."

Since he was a very skilled dancer of all the variations of the Texas two-step, she was delighted. She mentioned that. "Since you're bound and determined to dance every single dance with me, I must say that I'm thankful you know how."

Tom guessed, "So Garth can't dance?"

And she was caught. She blushed and squirmed and was too well-bred to agree that was so.

Tom had the slender, nothing, pocket-size little Swiss camera. He took pictures. There was no discernible flash.

The dance lasted late. It was a good time. Tom was used to meeting masses of people. He'd been practiced in that all his life. So he remembered names and connections. He was cheerful and humorous and the women, especially, really liked him. His attention to

Susan Lee did cause some stiffness in the female responses, since he was a stranger and she didn't share. And in turn, the male population disliked having a stranger catch the attention of Susan Lee.

As for Susan, she had a marvelous time! She laughed and flirted with Tom and danced too much and became smiling and sleepy.

So Tom said, "It's time to go home. I can't have you out on your feet. You're a wild and woolly woman."

In the darkness of the barn and in that noisy mob, she stretched up her slender arms in an exceptionally feminine way and yawned, ducking her head and laughing. The barn was so filled with humans that it had become quite warm, and her dress was a little sweat damp.

Tom watched his woman with hot eyes and smiled and smiled and smiled.

Four

When they left the barn dance, Tom was discreet in their goodbyes. Susan Lee noted that. Tom didn't want anyone aware of how long it would be before he took her home, and he didn't want anybody following them.

Guiding her through the crowd, his hand loved the feel of the damp cloth at her waist, but once they were outside he put his jacket on her before he put her into his car. He couldn't have her chilled.

And he drove on off. Naturally he didn't take the direct route. Someone could be leaving at the same time and inadvertently follow them. He put on a wicked saxophone tape and was silent. But his glances went over to her. She was pleasantly tired and she'd had a good time. She was relaxed back with her head resting on the back of the seat.

She looked wonderful.

Finally she asked, "*Now* where're we going?"

"How can you tell?"

"This is Mr. Frederick's fence. He always puts two strands on top."

"Why does he do that?"

"He's peculiar."

That sounded logical.

So he took his foot off the accelerator and moved it over to the brake, slowing the car to pull off the road.

"What's the matter?"

"I'm gonna kiss you, and I can't drive and cope with that much excitement at the same time."

"Oh, no."

"Oh, yes. I want to show you what happens to me if you should kiss me. I might not be able to handle a kiss. I don't want you going down the highway in a runaway car, with you trying to push my dead body away from the wheel before you crash."

"You are strange."

"Actually, I'm not. It's all you TEXANS who are a little out of step with the rest of the country. Okay. Brace yourself, I'm going to kiss you."

"You're not supposed to do that now."

"Why not?"

"Well, it's too soon. I've known you for—" she looked at her watch in the light from the dashboard "—for maybe, umm, about nine hours, all told, and you aren't supposed to kiss a strange woman that soon."

"So you admit to being strange?"

She explained, "To you."

"It will surprise you when I tell you that I agree with you. You are strange. So strange, and your impact is so powerful on men that the government knows about you and has sent me here to investigate you." He breathed deeply about five times while she sputtered; then he very skillfully unbuckled his and then her seat belt. He put his hands under her armpits, lifted her and turned her around so that she was face-to-face with him, and he kissed her.

It was spectacular.

All sorts of remarkable thrills and shivers took place. There was a roaring in their ears and they were buffeted by the erotic winds of passion.

She became soft and inert, and he turned to steel. He lifted his mouth slowly, and in the sudden silence there were the little sounds of their parting lips. It shivered his libido... hers, too. The entire experience was paralyzing.

They sat there immobile, gasping, breathing harshly, recovering. And the night birds began to sing. He managed to croak the word in some astonishment, "Listen!"

She was incapable of response.

He strained to speak in order to share the amazement. "That's a mockingbird singing."

With her eyelids closed and her lips pale, she struggled to kick start her vocal cords so that she could tell him, "Disturbed birds sing on occasion. That kiss—"

"They weren't singing before." He was awed.

She regrouped. "We were driving with the windows open, and the rushing of the wind covered the twitterings of the night birds."

He frowned down at her. "How can you be that logical after we just shared our first kiss?"

Pale, her eyes still closed, her body limp, she mumbled, "I wasn't affected by it."

So, of course, he kissed her again. Moving her malleable body and sneaking in some tricky touches.

After he lifted his mouth in that same sensual manner, with myriad, tiny, intimate sounds, she put her hands to her hair and erratically combed her feeble fingers through it in an effort to be casual. Still unable to open her eyes all the way, she tilted her head a little so that she could look at him, and she said, "Thank you for bringing me home."

His heart soared. He licked his lips and his wicked eyes lighted as he watched her paw around for her purse. Her skirt was up to the tops of her thighs. She leaned forward toward her door and fumbled for the handle. She managed to open the door by pushing it with her feet, and she mumbled, "G'bye."

He looked beyond her to the moon-highlighted fence posts and the mesquite trees that crowded them. He mentioned, "We aren't there yet."

"We aren't . . . where?"

"To your house. You'll have to kiss me again when we get there."

She said the word carefully, "No."

He was a bit indignant. "Why not?"

She mumbled, "I don't dare."

Tom was paralyzed. Finally he opened his car door and carefully got out.

She mumbled, "Don't leave me here alone."

"I won't. I just have to lift the back of the car a little."

"Are we stuck?"

"Not yet."

"You're not planning on driving me over there in that quicksand and getting your car stuck for the night and ruining my reputation, are you?"

"Is that a hopeful tone?"

She sputtered.

He sighed with his disappointment and replied in a disgruntled manner, "Well, then, not this time."

He went and worked on lifting the back end of the car. To reveal how awed she was by him, she clutched the sides of her seat for balance when she thought he lifted it. He didn't, actually.

Silently he got back into the car.

"You did that very smoothly. I wasn't jostled."

"Did...what?"

"Lifted the back end of the car."

She was an innocent. She hadn't understood his plight. He said, "I only aim to please you."

She snorted for the third time.

He complained, "If we should make this test and get married, are you gonna snort at me all the rest of my life?"

"I have to finish my doctorate."

He gasped and looked at her in some annoyance. "In what?"

"Real Texans would say 'What in'."

Obediently he responded, "What in?" But he couldn't resist saying, "That ends in a preposition, and Yankees shun doing that there."

"'Course." She agreed.

"If you will recall, I inquired politely—wanting to know—are you gonna snort at me all the rest of my life?"

"I'll see."

"That doesn't sound like a firm commitment to the eradication of faults."

"I said I'd consider it?" That was a do-you-understand statement.

"Snorting at a man is uncouth. If you can't pledge to eliminate doing that, I'm going to have to reconsider you."

"Good."

He sighed with a stunning show of patience. "I'll just have to wait and see?"

"Yep."

"Are you gonna kiss me good-night, or are you gonna walk home?"

With some sass, she told him, "I suppose you'll just have to wait and find out."

"You're recovering."

"Yep."

"What is your doctorate?"

"Quirky behavior in males."

"I don't believe it. I've never heard anything about that. It isn't a subject for a thesis."

"Oddly, it's never been explored. Probably because until lately the halls of learning have been controlled by... men. I'm breaking new ground."

"Why don't you do one on women?"

"It would be too diminishing for men to realize how truly intelligent women are. It isn't women who start wars."

"Helen of Troy?"

"Again, a man stole her and another went after them. Men have never adjusted to women being so superior mentally. That's why men go to such lengths to show women that they are really something because they are physically stronger."

He nodded. "We like attention."

"And, of course, they've spent a whole lot of time writing critiques about women. Being one, I know that women are logical and understandable. They wouldn't be a good study because they are stable. It's men who need to be studied, so that we can help them."

"Yeah?" He settled down to argue.

"Yeah."

"Well," he considered carefully. "I might be able to hunt down a quirky man for you. How much time do I have to get that done?" He was being helpful.

"I was considering *you* as the subject example. However, it may well be that you're in the lower percentile, and no one would believe the thesis." She gave him a really superior, snubbing regard.

He laughed. He did try not to, but his laughter bubbled and refused to subside. His eyes brimmed with his humor.

Unfortunately she smiled. Natural humor is so catching. A child's laughter gives no quarter, it is so spontaneous. So was Tom's.

She tried covering her mouth with a hand for a fake cough to conceal her response, but it wasn't successful. He reached a big hand over and waggled her head. "You're a gem." He told her that as if she were a collectible.

He said, "I think you can kiss me again if you're very, very careful."

"You've had your quota for the evening. And more than that for the time lapse of our acquaintance."

He looked thoughtful as he licked his lips and tucked his lower lip under his top teeth. "You're practicing the language you'll use in the thesis, right?"

"I speak that way."

"Like a thesis?"

"Like a woman."

"The bottom line is . . . are you going to give me another kiss or are you walking home?"

"That's blackmail!"

He considered that idea and bobbed his head a couple of times before he said, "Yeh."

"If there should ever be another encounter, I shall have my own car."

"Don't you like kissing me? If that's so, there could be serious ramifications."

"You are quite skilled. That indicates you've had practice." She condemned him with a serious look.

"You're the teacher."

"Hah!"

"I like 'hahs' better than snorts."

There was a silence. It was cozy in the car. The mockingbird was still singing sleepily. The night air was like wine. The moon was full and the grasses, the exposed leaves and branches and fence wires were silvered. Even the car rated a marvelous gleaming coating of moonlight. It was magical.

He mentioned, "It would be better if you kissed me now and let me take you home, because this is so peaceful and pretty that I might go to sleep waiting. I would doubt that you could move me enough so you could drive home."

"I'd just get out, go around and open your door. Then I'd get back in on this side and push you out with my feet."

"And leave me helpless on the road? You're heartless!"

"Well, I couldn't push you over this way, because I'd never get your legs over the console, and I'd probably spill your cup of water to boot."

"That would be sloppy. So you might just as well give me a kiss."

She considered that. "I could probably spare a very small one."

"That would be a start."

She looked over in censure. "You said 'one.'"

"But I had a big squishy one in mind. I don't want only a tiny, thin-lipped one."

"You didn't specify what kind. You only said 'a kiss'."

"Yeah. You're right. I flubbed it. What kind are you willing to share?"

She explained, "Since I'm exhausted from hauling you around the dance floor all evening, teaching you the steps, I suppose I can give you one small kiss."

He chided, "So grudging!"

"Yeah."

He settled back. "I need something that's dream material."

"I'm incapable."

"Hah! If you're 'incapable,' who was that who whammied me twice now?"

"Your imagination?"

"I couldn't have imagined you carrying on that-away and squeaking and wiggling to get closer and—"

She waited. Then she turned her head to look at him. He was looking out the windshield. She turned quickly and looked, too. Nothing. She asked in a whisper, "What are you seeing? Is someone out there?"

"The moon."

"Oh."

"Ready?"

She questioned, "Are you sure about this?"

"Yes."

She specified, "A small one."

"Okay."

She closed her eyes and lifted her pinched mouth.

He reached over, lifted her around again and settled her the way he wanted her. And he kissed her again. Their cells melted and sloshed around and their brains buzzed. Chaos. Physical disaster.

When he finally lifted his mouth from hers, she again lay limp across his body. His big hand rubbed soothingly up and down her back. His shoulder held her head. His other hand was not where it was supposed to be.

Her eyes were again closed. And yet again, she was inert. She formed the words slowly. "Cut that out."

"What." He encouraged her.

"That hand."

"This one?" He rubbed it on her back.

"The other one."

He slid the other down to her stomach to swirl there and then moved it slowly back up under her breast, pushing it up.

She managed to say, "That one."

He took her breast into his big hand and kneaded it slowly. "This one?"

"Cut it out."

"I like doing that."

She was silent. Her eyes still closed.

"Have you gone to sleep?"

"Quit."

"Quit . . . what?"

"Moving that hand around."

So he stopped kneading the mound and just held it. She said, "Move it."

He began kneading again.

"Off."

He slid it from her breast, down her stomach and around to her bottom.

She struggled enough, saying, "You're a lecher."

"Yeah."

Her eyes popped open. "You *admit* it?"

He shrugged. "To you. No one's listening. And if you tell, I'll just deny it. Being a man, everyone will know I'm telling the truth."

"I'll put that in my thesis."

"So you're going to research me after all? Unbutton my shirt."

She enunciated carefully, "Research . . . your *brain!*"

"Wanna know what I'm thinking right now?"

"No."

"I'm gonna get you, Susan Lee McCrea."

"No."

"Yep. And since you finally gave me a decent kiss, I'll—"

"That was *decent?*"

"Yeah."

"I hesitate to ask what you think is inflammatory."

He confessed, "I don't know. You haven't kissed me thataway . . . yet."

She gasped. "What did you think *that* one was?"

"I've forgotten. You mean like this?"

And darned if he didn't do the same thing all over again.

Her hands pawed at him and she made little sounds.

He lifted his mouth from hers and his hands moved without moving. He asked huskily, "What do you want?"

"Let . . . go."

"How can you be that coherent?"

"Please. Let . . . go."

So reluctantly he began to release her. It took a while. He had to slowly rub his face into the space where her neck met her shoulder. His whiskers were budding and it was excessively erotic. And he had to gain control of his hands because they moved around and he lost track of where they were supposed to be. He explained all that quite earnestly.

He finally lifted his hands from her and said, "You're free." And he waited.

She had to gird her loins to lift herself from his body and rearrange herself over onto her side of the front seat. It was a trying thing to accomplish. She persevered.

He complained, "You kiss me like that and then you want me to drive this car all by myself?"

"Can't you?"

"Hardly."

"Maybe I can. Where's the key?"

"In the ignition."

She reached over and turned it on.

He inquired in a rather irritated manner, "You plan to drive this car from over there?"

"Yeah. I don't dare to sit on your lap."

He could see the wisdom of what she said, but his lap got really, really excited by just the idea. He said, "I'll drive."

"Do you know where we are, or how to get to my house?"

"Aren't you going home with me?"

"Good gravy, Tom, you know better than that!"

"I'm going with you? Do your parents mind? Your dad didn't seem too welcoming to—"

"No. We're taking me home, and then you go back to Petersons' house. You're staying there."

"Yeah." In a disgruntled manner he went on, "I can't see how you can be that organized in your thinking, after kissing me that way."

"That's why I'm the one doing the thesis."

He draped an arm over the steering wheel as he turned his head and studied her.

She sat primly, smoothing her skirt down over her knees and looking around rather busily in multiple tiny turns of her head while moving her mouth in great indifference to him.

He was one of Felicia Brown's actual children, so he sighed hugely for a large audience of one, and he said, "Go ahead, act independent. Your time is limited. Do all that while you can."

"You're going to—control me?" She tilted her head back and gave him a challenging look.

"You won't mind." He put the car into gear and turned around on the deserted road in order to head back.

He arrived at her house in due time, and he eased the car to a hushed stop. He said, "Now."

She smiled with her hand on the door handle and said, "The dance was fun. You're really quite good. Thank you for advancing my study. Good night."

He opened his own door and met her at the hood of the car. "Browns always see women to their doors."

As she hurried her steps, she looked around at the moon-washed countryside and said, "I'm fine."

He corrected her wordage, "You're spectacular."

She waved a denying hand to disperse such elaboration. "No. I'm another ordinary woman. We are all spectacular." She hesitated for emphasis, then said, "Especially to men who want something from us."

"Want something?" He matched her steps going up onto her porch. He asked politely, "Want—what?"

She gestured with that talented hand, to indicate the enormity of it all. "Socks washed, meals cooked, papers printed, kisses, th—"

"You've hit it!" So, of course, since she had mentioned it, he enclosed her, pulling her tightly against his urgent body and he gave her another one of those kind of kisses. And it was just like the others.

Her soft body melted against his stone one, his arms were iron bands, his mouth was greedy. His big hand supported her wobbly head against the pressure of his kiss. She swooned. Her mouth was parted like a baby bird's and his fed on it.

When Tom finally released Susan Lee and set her pawing hands away, she fell back against the wall of the porch and was a wrecked, boneless mass.

He was a dithering tangle of nerves and jerky movements. He looked around reorienting himself, and he said, "I'll call you."

She nodded.

He panted and swallowed and seemed a little hyper. He said, "Is the door locked?"

She shook her head.

He opened the screen door and held it. She didn't move. He closed the door and stood there. She didn't want to go inside? She wanted to be outside with...him? He wasn't sure he could handle another of the kisses and still cling reasonably to the Brown code of conduct.

He asked, "Do you want to stay out here with me?"

She shook her head.

He figured it out. "Need some help getting inside?"

She nodded.

He opened the door, and his hands helped her get inside. She didn't look back, she just kept on walking. She turned and said in a mumble, "Close the door."

Was he supposed to close it and stay outside or was he supposed to follow her inside? He waited, breathing brokenly.

She turned again and said, "G'night." And she went on off into a hallway.

Oh.

He was to go back to Petersons'. How was he going to do that? If he went there and jogged down the lane and back, the dogs would all go with him. So he drove over to where the lost dog had been and looked around, carrying the rifle.

How did the creatures all vanish so silently that he never knew anything was there? They were all asleep. He was the only animal awake and restless.

He knew they could all smell him. He'd sweat while he'd danced with Susan and he'd sweat again but differently with her kisses. A sexual sweat. The animals all were probably "reading" his frustration and snickering over him. He smiled at the night, sharing the humor.

Far off, he heard a coyote howl. He knew the feeling. He'd like to lean back his head and howl, too.

So he did. He howled to express his frustration—and over his delight that frustration was possible. He howled at that huge, magic moon. He silenced the whole area.

He stood in the night, in the middle of nowhere, and grinned as he looked around the empty thicket. He looked up at the miracle of the moon, at the endless sky and the mysteries that it still held.

He looked at his world. Then he gave thanks for his life. For the meeting with such a frustrating woman. And for the opportunity to *be* frustrated, with the hope of solving it. He walked around the peopleless area as if he were king of the mountain and could solve anything.

He went back to his car, drove to the Petersons' and quietly climbed the stairs to his room. Shoeless, he went to the closest bath and showered. Then he went to bed to survive intensely vivid dreams.

The next morning, Tom opened his eyes and looked out the windows at another beautiful day. The sun was rising, the birds were busy, there were sounds of the animals.

He smiled at the world, and remembering his howling the night before, he smiled at himself. He stretched and felt great.

And he had those rolls of film to process.

He got out of bed, dressed in jeans and a shirt, pulled on his boots and went down to a huge breakfast. Willy was cooking, but the rolls were Mim's.

In the shed, Tom used quite a bit of paper because he enlarged all the prints. He discarded several that were unkind, but the rest he would give to Susan Lee. She could pass them on to the subjects, if she chose.

And he printed extra copies of those of Susan Lee. He looked at the prints and smiled back at her. She was a jewel. She was so free. Her laugh was like honey to his ears—sweet and melting.

How could he possibly be in love this soon? Was it only want? He narrowed his eyes as he looked at his best picture of her. Was she that special? How could he question? She was wonderful. Perfect.

He put most of those of Susan Lee aside and carried the rest in to Mim.

Mim went through the snapshots in great delight. She told family histories of all those shown and how they were related and what position their families held in that area. And she identified the men who wanted Susan Lee.

Mim asked, "How come you got to take Susan Lee to the barn dance? I thought Garth Pippins had the inside track with her."

"Naw. Not him."

Mim did push a little. "How'd you get to take her to the dance?"

"When you're older and can handle it better, I'll tell you."

That made Mim very alert and watching. Mim's eyes sparkled and she became intensely interested, but she didn't demand an explanation right then.

That showed why Sam Fuller had been so right in selecting the Petersons for Tom. Sam hadn't wanted Tom to be the subject of relentless cross-examinations. In that sparse community, everyone knew everyone else and curiosity ran rampant.

Mim could just about control hers.

Of course, Mim told Geo to inquire as to how come Tom escorted Susan Lee to the barn dance. And Geo's attention was caught.

Geo got to see the pictures at noon. He did look at them because there were some of Tommy and Mim, and one of him on the hospital floor when he fainted. Being the man he was, it didn't bother him at all that there were pictures of him out cold on the floor that way.

After lunch, when they'd left the table and were outside, and just like it was off the top of his head, Geo asked Tom, "How come you got to take Susan Lee to that barn dance?"

Tom looked off to the edge of the world, resettled his Stetson in the studied way he'd learned and said the shutout reply, "I don't think you have time right now to hear all about that."

And Geo laughed.

Five

It was about then that Geo mentioned, "Somebody's coming down the lane."

Tom asked, "How do you know that?"

"The buzzards flapped up a little bit just above the trees. They do that when you drive by too fast. Somebody's in a hurry."

Logically Tom asked, "What're the buzzards after?"

"A possum."

With amused patience, Tom asked, "Now, how do you know it's a possum?"

"I went out and looked this morning. I get up at a reasonable time." He turned his head and gave Tom a superior look. "I don't loll around in the bed like some guest."

Tom scoffed. "You didn't go to the barn dance."

"That is true."

Before Geo could get around to inquiring—again—about how Tom had managed to go with Susan Lee, Tom asked, "Expecting somebody?"

"No. That's why I'm standing here exchanging light conversation with you. So's I can see who it is."

Bravely Tom promised, "I'll back you."

Geo looked tolerant and licked his lips instead of prolonging the useless chatter.

As the car came into sight, Geo said, "I guess it's for you. That's Garth Pippins's car."

"Uh-oh." Tom smiled.

"Trouble?"

"Nothing I can't handle."

"Well, then, I'll just back off and watch. Make it good. I have a reputation to preserve."

Garth pulled up in a circle so that the driver's side was away from Tom. Garth shut off the motor, opened the door and got out with deliberation.

Tom loved it when people were predictable.

Garth went around to the front of his car and leaned his hip against the hood. He nodded to Geo and fixed Tom with a stern look.

Since Tom had seen Garth only driving or leaning on or standing by his car, it wasn't too much to figure the car was important to Garth and gave him a feeling of power. Tom slouched in the most macho way he could devise while not having a car to lean against.

Garth pointed at Tom with his chin and said, "I'd like a word with you."

Geo folded his arms on his chest and stood with his feet planted as he watched Garth.

Tom was courteous. "Only one word? What's that?"

"That note was meant for you."

Tom considered and said, "That's a whole sentence." But his voice was soft with warning.

Geo looked at Tom differently and shifted to stand easier.

Garth squinted his eyes and put his head forward a little as he said in a deadly voice, "You fooled with me and Susan Lee."

And Tom smiled.

Garth got a little red around his neck, and he said again, "She wrote that note to you!"

"But it worked with giving it to you."

Geo was looking from one to the other in such an interested manner.

Garth said in a huff, "You leave Susan Lee alone. Do you hear me?"

Tom spread his arms out from his sides in a helpless way and replied, "I've got the same problem you have, Garth."

"I don't have no problem."

"Well, good. Then there isn't one."

"What you talking about, boy?"

"I thought you were partial to that lady."

And Garth burst out rudely, "I am!"

"Well," Tom was logical. "So'm I? So we have the same problem."

"I've been courting Susan Lee for over six months."

Tom listened courteously and waited.

With the silence, Garth was forced to say, "She belongs to me."

"Well, does she know that?"

"We've been going around all this time."

"Maybe she didn't have any other choice until recently."

And Garth said, "I want you to stay away from her. Do you understand me?"

"Sorry, Garth, I'm hooked. May the best man win her."

"Watch out, boy, you're asking for trouble."

Tom shrugged his shoulders. "What will be, will be." He pushed. "I can't embarrass my hosts and tangle here." Peripherally he saw Geo's surprised and indignant start. Tom went on, "Want to meet somewheres else?"

"There won't be no need for that. I've told you what I want you to do, and if you're smart you'll pay attention."

Tom countered, "Well . . ."

But Garth turned away, pulled open the door of his car, flung himself into it and roared away with a splattering of gravel and dirt.

When they finished laughing, Geo asked, "What note?"

"Susan Lee wrote me a note saying for me to go on home and not wait around for her." Then Tom advised Geo kindly. "I'd suggest that you save that bit of information and tell Mim at some really appropriate time when you want points."

"You are a crafty man. Just mention to me why she wrote that note and how you got it to Garth instead?"

"The note didn't have my name on it, but she'd signed hers to it. So I discarded the envelope and folded the note and gave it to Garth, who was waiting in the parking lot to take her home."

Impressed, Geo was admiring. "How'd you think of doing that?"

"Well, it was just so obvious! And it worked."

"Sam Fuller never mentioned you were sly."

"He knows Tweed, who's just about the best of the Browns, and he's met Salty. He and Felicia stayed with Sam Fuller for a while. They're upright and honest. Of course, Tweed was only with us for a couple of years. And I'm one of the actual Brown children, so Sam figured I was open and honest, too."

Geo nodded to indicate he understood. "You are really something. What did Susan Lee do when she found out what you'd done?"

"I told her about it right away. She was shocked, but I distracted her by taking her to see Dog. And she didn't mind going to the dance with me. Garth wasn't there."

"So somebody told him you were there with Susan Lee."

"Probably half the people there did that. He had a burr under his tail."

"He's gonna push. You got to know that."

Tom nodded a couple of bobs. "It is probable."

"You know how to handle him?"

"I grew up with about fifty other kids around. Salty wouldn't let us do anything dirty or underhanded, but we did wrestle, and on occasion we did fight." Tom took a step and then looked at Geo. "So, you think he'll want to fight."

"Maybe so."

"So."

"He's got a pound or two on you."

"My arms are longer."

"You've already considered that?"

"Yes. Since the first time I walked Susan Lee out of the hospital and saw him standing beside his car waiting for her. Do you suppose he sleeps in it?"

"Might."

Tom laughed such a wonderful, low male sound of confidence that Geo slapped his shoulder as he, too, laughed. "I want to be there."

"If I'm allowed a second, I'll name you."

"I don't think Garth would gang up on you."

"Salty taught us how to handle even that."

"No! How?"

"You take out the cowards first."

"You're right. Gangs are made up of guys that don't know how to run by themselves. I'll teach the boys. I've been remiss."

Tom tasted the unusual word for a TEXAN. "Remiss—"

Geo elaborated, "Overlooked a serious, little detail."

"The reason Salty knew to teach us that was because we were such a hodgepodge of kids. My parents raised twenty-eight kids, but they took in a whole slew of part-time kids that needed shelter. Tweed was one."

"I'd like to know Salty."

"And Felicia. They're a team."

"Get 'em down here sometime. And, Tom, count me in on any problem."

"Thanks."

Inside, Tom called Susan Lee on the phone. His voice warm and husky, he said, "Good morning, darling."

She ignored the endearment and replied hotly, "Garth was here. He was furious that you took me to the barn dance."

Verbally unwinding and becoming her advocate, Tom asked in quick surprise that was nicely indignant, "What'd he say?"

"He said he was surprised at me. That's what he said. Can you believe that? He said my parents hadn't raised me very well—at all—for me to act so unlady-like!"

Tom loved it, but not obviously. He gave her his nicely structured shock. "He said that to you? What did you say to him?"

"I couldn't actually call him a snot—"

His agreement was sympathetic. "That's not what a lady would say."

"So I told him to go blow his nose."

Fighting his hilarity, Tom managed a serious tone. "What'd he say then?"

"I don't know. I hung up."

"'Course you did. That's what you should have done right away. As soon as—"

"He never gave me any chance to explain!"

Tom assured her, "He's uncouth."

"Actually, it was you who did all this. Got Garth stirred up and cross with me."

Tom was on her side. "His conduct today showed his true colors. He doesn't deserve you."

"That note—"

"It was just the thing to reveal the real Garth Pikkins, who is—"

She interrupted, "His name is Pippins."

"Oh, yes. He's just so picky that I missaid the name. You've made a lucky escape."

"His feelings were hurt."

That comment from Susan Lee made Tom's scalp tense. "Did he say that?"

"He said I wasn't a lady and—"

"You're the most gentle and well-bred lady I've ever—"

"He was shocked by my conduct."

"Have you been conducting yourself out of character? Is this something I need to know about? Come on, Susan Lee, you are one of the most gentle women I've ever known."

"How can you tell?" Her voice was brittle.

"I compare you to the most skilled lady I know, my mother Felicia."

"I'm like a woman who is over fifty?"

"No. You're like you. You're special. Contrasted to Felicia, you're a beginning lady."

"So you believe that I need some disciplining, too?" Her voice was stilted and sharp.

In his most sincere tone, Tom assured her, "You're the most gracious lady and the kindest I've ever seen. All you need is some years."

"You have that great a backlog of women?"

"None," his voice was sincere.

"You couldn't be as smooth as you are unless you've had a great deal of practice."

Tom could recognize a gauntlet. If he wasn't really careful, he'd be out on his ear with Garth. He said, "I'll be right over."

He hung up on her instant protest, "N—"

The phone rang instantly.

Tom was running down the stairs and he yelled, "I'm not here!"

He sprinted through the house to get to his car and explained in passing Mim, "I've got to put out a brush fire."

Mim was yelling for Geo and the hands as Tom slammed into his own car and almost stripped the gears getting it started. He looked for kids, saw none and roared out of the parking area and down the Petersons' lane.

So when he arrived at the McCreas', Mrs. McCrea looked startled and said, "How come you're not to the brush fire? Where is it?"

"Here."

She looked around in fast jerks. "Where?"

"Your daughter is planning to bolt."

Mrs. McCrea was astounded. "With *Garth?*"

"He's trying."

Mrs. McCrea misheard his word and responded, "I find him tedious, too. But who can tell about a man with a woman? He must have something to recommend him."

"No," Tom assured her gently.

"But what about the brush fires? Aren't you going to help? The Petersons have bragged on how you pitch in. Brush fires are very fast around here."

"What brush fire?"

"The one you're running to put out!" She looked at him in an annoyed way, and she was too obvious in the fact that she didn't think he was working with a full deck.

"I'm putting out the brush fire of Susan Lee's withdrawing from me."

"Oh . . . Well. She might. However, right now you have to get on the phone and tell everybody there isn't any—"

The phone in the house rang.

He could hear Susan Lee answering it. She said, "Not here. No. He just came up on the porch. No. I'm not speaking to him. You may do that yourself!"

Susan Lee apparently put the phone aside because she called to her mother in a very formal way, "If the

Brown person should come past here, the fire brigade would like to speak with him.''

To Tom, Mrs. McCrea said, ''I believe she means to tell you the phone call is for you.''

''Is she always this way?''

Mrs. McCrea gave him a patient sigh and replied, ''Only since meeting you.''

Tom smiled. ''I'm making progress.''

''Your yardstick is out of kilter.''

''Brace yourself. She loves me.''

''I believe you have your work cut out for you. Do answer the phone. Whoever is calling you is speaking so loudly that I can hear him clear out here. A woman would never conduct her phone calls in that manner.''

''Your daughter is very like you.''

Mrs. McCrea smoothed up the back of her hair to her bun and said, ''She'd need a lot of years before she can claim that.''

Tom laughed.

Mrs. McCrea gave him a very smug and wicked smile.

So Tom was let into the house and directed to the telephone. Susan Lee had disappeared.

Tom picked up the phone and mentioned, ''This is Tom Brown.''

Then he had to remove the phone from his ear in order to hear what was being yelled. There were motors in the background and people hollering.

''This is Fire Chief Clyde Burton. Where the hell's the fire?''

Naturally Tom inquired, ''What fire?''

''What d'yo' say?''

And Tom yelled back, ''What fire?''

''The brush fire you told Mim about?''

"That only concerned a personal issue."

"Your kids?"

"No kids. My business."

"The fire's on your land? When did you get la—"

Now, how was Tom going to explain himself without involving Susan Lee? He put his hand over the mouthpiece and hissed at Mrs. McCrea, "If you would consider that I might become your son-in-law, go outside and start a brush fire, or my goose is cooked."

So Susan Lee came into the room with her big eyes on Tom, and she asked her mother, "Why is someone going to cook his goose?"

Her mother went on past her as she replied, "By now, probably most of the county."

Then Susan Lee looked directly at Tom and asked, "What have you done?"

"It was a misunderstanding."

"About... me?"

"Partly." She might as well share the blame. A stranger would be censored much harsher than a delicate native like her.

He said, "Let's call a truce until this is settled. I could be drawn and quartered, or I might even be put in jail."

"Why?"

It was understandable that she would ask that. "It's all your fault."

"What?" Her attention was caught and she was speaking to him and looking at him as if he was an actual part of the human race.

He explained, "When you were telling me about Pipper's visit—"

"Pippins."

"Yeah, his visit. I found myself in a very awkward place. So I—"

"You were at the Petersons'. Are they fed up with you, too?"

"No, no. They like me just like everybody else likes me."

"Did you set the fire?"

"What fire?"

"The entire telephone system is on alert to some brush fires you're attending."

"You're the brush fire."

"Nonsense."

"I went past Mim. She wanted to know what was all the rush, and I just said I had to put out a brush fire."

"No one jokes around here about something so serious as a brush fire. The wind lifts them along and they are a disaster. You'll be tarred and feathered." She appeared to take some comfort in the idea.

Tom boshed, "That's just for carpetbaggers."

She accused, "You're a Yankee."

"Well, I didn't set any brush fires and I didn't say there were any... except for you. You scare me spitless. Don't go cool and distant on me."

She replied snootily, "I'll bring you cookies in jail."

"You don't believe me?" He squinted his eyes and frowned in disbelief.

"Where's Mother?"

"I sent her out to start a brush fire and save my skin."

"You're a pyromaniac?"

"*You're* the brush fire, you hot little tamale. You're scorching me! I'm about to burst in spontaneous combustion."

"You are angry because you tricked me and made Garth so mad?"

"I'm scared I could lose you."

"I think I should stick to Texans. They are at least understandable. You're peculiar."

"I'm perfectly logical."

"Then why are you holding the phone and allowing that irate Clyde Burton to yell like that?"

"Here. You tell him you're the brush fire."

She considered that. Then she said, "Go see if you can help my mother. I don't believe she's ever tried to start a brush fire before this."

He warned her, "Even if we don't work this out between us, I'm keeping your mother. She didn't snub me even once!"

His love flared her eyes and she retorted, "She collects strange people. If you don't believe me, ask Daddy."

"Just get the fire brigade off my back." He handed her the phone.

Mrs. McCrea came inside. Her clothing was dirty, her face smudged, her hair knot askew. She yelled at the top of her lungs, "Get the fire brigade! There's a brush fire!"

Tom grinned ear to ear. He said smugly to his love, "Your momma is a point in your favor, and right now you need all you can get."

They were out in the field working with wet gunnysacks when the fire brigade came roaring up, and by then, the fire had spread and they needed the help.

"Now, tell me, how'd this start?" Clyde frowned at Mrs. McCrea. "And where's your husband?"

"He went into town."

Clyde scowled, "He's never had a brush fire on his place. He's gonna wonder how it started."

"A spontaneous combustion?"

"In the middle of the field?" Clyde was offended by the very idea of spontaneous combustion on moist grass.

"I didn't see it start. I saw only the smoke."

"Well, I find this very suspicious. Is your daughter trying to call attention to herself?"

"By starting a fire in our own field?"

"How come that Tom Brown came hurtling over here before it even started?"

"Susan Lee was talking to him on the phone and saw the smoke?"

Clyde didn't know if that was a question or a questioning statement. He squinted his eyes at his wife's best friend and said, "When Brice gets home, he's gonna be curious and persistent."

Mrs. McCrea stepped back and put a smudged hand to her rounded, dirty shirtfront and exclaimed in soft shock, "You think the fire was set? Who would do such a dumb thing?"

"I been asking."

And Mrs. McCrea said, "Since it's taken this long, it's already afternoon. Have a cold beer and tell the people here how to vote."

That switched Clyde's interests, and he didn't ask any more questions.

A smudge-faced, tacky-clothed Tom didn't move his lips at all as he told his cohort, "I owe you."

She smiled like a tarnished and smudged angel, "Yes." And her tone was unpardonably smug.

"You want me to take that iron tire rim off your hands," he guessed as he solemnly nodded.

"Let's say I could possibly be on your side."

"Like I said, if your daughter and I don't make it, I'm keeping you as kin."

She looked off sideways over the blackened field and the still-flaming shed. She told the smudged and tattered Tom, "While you'll have to work for her to allow you to believe it, you've already won her."

Tom was shocked. "She's playing hard to get?"

His mother-in-law-to-be lowered her face, but her nose stayed lifted. "I thought you were smarter than you've just revealed."

A little irritated, Tom protested, "I am smart. I just never wanted a woman—before this—on a permanent basis and all."

"Don't you forget this day and this fire and how all this came about. To keep me silent, I'll extract all sorts of things for this day. . . from you."

Suspiciously he demanded, "What's your first name. I'll bet it's a jawbreaker, and you'll want a granddaughter named that. Tell me. Wait until I sit down, but tell me."

She was still toplofty and her eyebrows went up. "It's Janella."

"Why. . . that's not bad. We'll consider it."

"Not that." She dismissed it. But she elaborated, "Christmas here, every year."

He bargained, "Every other one. You haven't experienced anything like the Christmases up home in Ohio."

"It's cold up there."

Tom soothed her. "The house is big, so you could stay inside. But you might like sledding on the hill in back of the house."

Nostalgically Janella remembered, "I rode a sleigh in Switzerland through the snow."

"That was elegant. We'll figure out something for you."

Susan Lee came by the resting pair and gave them lemonade. "What are you talking about?"

"Christmas."

"Really." She was disbelieving. "What were you talking about?"

Tom frowned in censure. "What a difficult woman you are."

"My mother would never refer to me in that way—to a stranger."

Tom and Janella exchanged a quick, smiling glance.

Again Susan Lee asked, "What were you talking about?"

"Balky horses."

Susan Lee said, "Your horse isn't balky."

Tom replied, "Up in Ohio, we have a riderless pony."

"I could ride him."

"I'll lay you...a bet." He almost forgot the last two words, the first ones were so attention getting.

By then, the fire was just about out. There were some still watching the shed, but the field was no longer expanding the fire.

Most of the brushfire workers were drifting tiredly back to the house yard. There they lounged around, accepting cold bottles of beer and eating lunch from the staggering amount of food all the wives had brought to the McCreas' house.

The wives were saying things like, "I was so bored. Did you set the fire so we could have a picnic?"

Janella retorted, "Would I be dressed this way in these tacky clothes if I'd thought you all were going to have to be here?"

"You have a point," the questioner admitted.

"But wasn't it fun?" Janella laughed. "All the excitement!"

"Oh, did *you* set it?"

"Of *course* not. Don't be any sillier than you are."

They all settled down and no one else speculated on how the fire had started until Brice came home, but by then they were all so mellow and relaxed that no one paid any attention to his questions.

Tom cornered Susan Lee in the dark entryway and trapped her into giving him a kiss for all his help. She was prissy and turned her head a whole lot, but she didn't squirm away from him.

He asked her, "Did you set that fire to lure me over here?"

"Don't be an idiot. Why would I want you around?"

"Because you can't stand being away from me." He supplied that reason because he felt that way.

"I have to wash my hair."

"Why?"

She was patient. "From helping with the fire."

In a smoky voice, he told her, "You've started a fire in me. I'm about to burn up, wanting you."

"That's lust."

With her trapped against the wall by him, he assured her, "I recognized that."

"You're not suppose to say those things."

"I'm not?"

"No." She was still looking around, but she wasn't trying to get away, and her words were hushed so's not to call attention to them.

In his smoky voice, he asked, "What am I supposed to say?"

"That...that...I'm pretty."

"You're not pretty, you're gorgeous. You make my head swim and my heart go crazy. Feel me." And his tone was ragged.

She put her hand on his chest. "You have a good, strong heart."

"You're feeling the reverberation from inside your hand. My real heart's in your hand. You took it away from me last night out in the car."

"No." Her word was softly spoken and her eyes were enormous.

He was sweating. "Yeah. That's what happened, all right. You stole it. You could comfort me if you kissed me improperly."

In a whisper, she said, "I don't know how to kiss...improperly."

He denied that. "You kissed me thataway last night when we were parked out in the country. You've ruined me."

"I haven't done anything to you. How could I have ruined you?"

"You've ruined me for other women. You've riveted my attention to you. You lured me."

"I did not, either." But she was breathless, and she watched him so big eyed.

"You did it thisaway."

He put his hands low on her waist and brought her body to his as he leaned forward and kissed her so that the back of her head was against the wall and her hips were against the tops of his thighs.

She was shocked to feel his hardened sex against her stomach. He was very aroused. No other man had been that bold with her, and even as she returned his kiss, she blushed scarlet.

He growled low and dangerously, "Do you know now what you do to me?"

She had the boldness to reply, "You're easy."

"Well?"

"Well . . . what?"

"What are you going to do about me?"

She pushed back from him and moved her hips to indicate that he was to stop crowding her. "I hardly know you."

"You're getting close to knowing me. Do you realize that?"

"I'm not ready for—that. You have to go slower."

"I may die."

And she snorted.

PLAY "MATCH 3" – YOU COULD WIN UP TO A MILLION–$$$ IN LIFETIME INCOME (YES, $1,000,000!) –GET FREE BOOKS & AN EXCITING SURPRISE GIFT, TOO!

★ Did you complete the first 3 rows of your "Match 3" Game? Did you print your name & address on the Game? Are you also playing & enclosing your Bonus Games? Please do, because so doing definitely qualifies you for a chance to win one of the Fabulous Prizes being offered, up to & including a MILLION-$$$ in Lifetime Income!

★ Did you complete rows 4 & 5? If you did, you are entitled to Free Books & a really nice Surprise Gift, as your introduction to our Reader Service. The Service does not require you to buy, ever. When you get your Free Books, if you don't want any more, just write cancel on the statement & return it to us.

★ You can of course go for prizes alone by not playing rows 4 & 5. But why pass up such good things? Why not go for all the prizes you can - & why not get everything that's being offered & that you're entitled to? It's all free, yours to keep & enjoy. It's a "SURE FIRE" opportunity for you!

Free Books and Gift offer not valid to current Silhouette Desire® subscribers. OFFER LIMITED—1 "MATCH 3" play per envelope. All orders subject to approval.

© 1991 HARLEQUIN ENTERPRISES LTD.

PRINTED IN U.S.A.

Use These Stamps to Complete Your
"MATCH 3" Game

Simply detach this page & see how many matches you can find for your "MATCH 3" Game. Then take the matching stamps and stick them on the Game. Three-of-a-kind matches in rows 1 through 3 qualify you for a chance to win a Big Money Prize—up to a Million-$$$ ...

... THREE-OF-A-KIND-MATCHES IN ROWS 4 & 5 GETS YOU FREE BOOKS & A NICE SURPRISE GIFT AS WELL! PLAYING IS FREE - FUN - EASY & THE WAY YOU COULD WIN!

PLAY TODAY!

PLAY THIS
MATCH GAME 3

with Big Money Prizes—you could
WIN UP TO $1-MILLION!
get Free Books and Surprise Gift, too

	STICK 1st	STICK 2nd	STICK 3rd
MATCH 3 you are instantly eligible to **WIN $10,000**	MATCH HERE	MATCH HERE	MATCH HERE
MATCH 3 you are instantly eligible to **WIN $50,000**	MATCH HERE	MATCH HERE	MATCH HERE
MATCH 3 you are instantly eligible to **WIN $1-MILLION**	MATCH HERE	MATCH HERE	MATCH HERE
MATCH 3 and get **FOUR FREE BOOKS**	MATCH HERE	MATCH HERE	MATCH HERE
MATCH 3 and get **A GREAT SURPRISE GIFT**	MATCH HERE	MATCH HERE	MATCH HERE

▲ FOLD, REMOVE THIS BOTTOM PART, RETURN "MATCH 3" GAME PIECE ▲

THIS COULD BE THE LUCKIEST DAY OF YOUR LIFE
because your "MATCH 3" Game qualifies you for a chance to win a Big Money Prize—up to $1-MILLION in Lifetime Cash—for FREE! It's also your chance to get Free Books & an Exciting Free Surprise Gift with no obligation to buy anything, now or ever. Just find all the matching stamps you can, stick them on your Game, fill in your name & address on the other side & return your Game in the reply envelope provided. We'll take care of the rest!

CAREFULLY PRE-FOLD, TEAR ALONG DOTTED LINES, PLAY "MATCH 3" GAME & RETURN IN REPLY ENVELOPE PROVIDED

Six

"Poof!" Susan Lee summarily dismissed Tom dying of sexual frustration. "I—"

Her mother called, "Susan Lee! I could use some help with the lunch dishes in here." Her mother had called her name in four syllables.

Susan Lee told Tom, "Let me go."

"Just don't answer."

"Momma knows you've got me cornered here, and she's warning you that it's been long enough for us to be alone this way."

"How'd she know we're where we are?"

"Mothers keep track."

In some shock, Tom gasped, "Felicia did that. I can remember having to go and find one or another of my sisters when they had male company. I was supposed to ask if they wanted some lemonade or some such. Was that what my mother was doing?"

"All mothers do that. Let go."

"I suppose you'll be that same way with our daughters?"

"More than likely. Let me go."

"You've just admitted you're taken with me and we're going to make love enough to have daughters. Let's practice."

"I said nothing of the sort! Back off or you'll be embarrassed when Papa comes looking."

He groaned. "You feel so good against me."

"You're a lecher." She accused him yet again.

"Yeah." With great reluctance, he did manage to slowly release her. He stood away from her and put his hands into his pockets. He hunched his shoulders and stretched his arms down and breathed.

Susan Lee prissily tidied her hair and straightened her clothing just as her father called, "Hey, Susan Lee? You and Tom want some lemonade?"

She whispered, "See? It's the same the world over." Then she called, "Thanks, Daddy, but not right now."

Tom growled down low and deep, "I'm thirsty."

She turned her body and lifted her head as she opened her mouth to recall her refusal, but he stopped her. In that low, sexy roughness, he told her, "I need some really wet kisses."

She glanced up at his face, and her mouth opened for her gasp. Then she said, "Why, Mr. Brown, how you do go on!"

Since her shock was so fake, he laughed in his throat.

Busily she moved in tiny ways as she told him, "I need to go help Momma so she can see that I'm still pure."

"I'll go out the other door." He smiled a tiny bit, but his eyes were hot and amused by her.

"Would you like me to bring you some lemonade?"

"Heck, I was gonna ask for another beer so's you could see the real Tom Brown."

"No, that wouldn't do at all. We're really a very unsophisticated community clear out here."

Tom laughed.

She said, "I don't know why you'd laugh that way. Just who've you been around?"

"Honey, I've lived down in these here parts for over eight years. As you all say, you can't fool a TEXAS boy."

She replied snippily, "I'll bring you some lemonade. That'll throw Momma for a loop."

He watched her busily walk away from him through the double doors into the living room, on beyond through the dining room and out of sight. She was something.

He took a little time before he went outside into the afternoon light and confronted the collective attention of the relaxed and well-fed fire brigade. By then, they all knew he'd taken Susan Lee to the barn dance the night before. They'd either been at the dance or they'd heard it mentioned. Susan Lee had been with Tom Brown . . . not Garth Pippins.

Having spent the whole morning fighting his future mother-in-law's fire, Tom was so soot covered and tired that he looked like a hero. The women smiled at him and offered him cold beer.

Susan Lee was bringing him lemonade when that was offered. Remembering what Tom had said about how he would act after the second beer, Susan Lee asked with caution, "Haven't you already had one?"

Tom rose from his squat among the lounging men. His eyelashes closed down, almost covering the wickedness of his glance, and he asked, "Worried?"

She got very snippy and replied, "I just didn't want you to embarrass the older ladies here. They aren't used to pushy Yankees."

"Honey, I've been here over a trillion five minutes. Five minutes is all it takes to be a TEXAN. So I'm a real one, by now, and I can't be labeled a Yankee."

"I'm sixth-generation TEXAN." She gave him the aloof, head-tilted-back snubbing that declaration called for.

He said without any emphasis at all, "Glory be."

She instructed him, "A trillion-five-minute native does *not* a sixth generationer make."

He loved it. "Our kids will be half-breeds."

"Who says we'll be having any? You're taking a precious lot for granted."

He growled the words just for her ear, "You don't kiss indifferent."

And she blushed. Her chin went down, her eyelids covered her eyes and she blushed. He loved it.

Some hunky old man drawled, "What you tellin' that chile, boy, to make her blush thataway?"

Smooth as silk, that ex-Yankee Tom replied, "I told her she's pretty."

A grizzled old man then said, "Hell, she's knowed that since she was two and her daddy didn't drown her."

That got a chuckle.

Another settled man asked, "You serious about that one?"

Tom considered as he watched Susan Lee's blush deepen. He said thoughtfully, "I'll have to see if she can plow with a mule and shoe a horse."

The old man puffed, "That ain't no trial a'tall!"

Tom went on as if he had planned to all along, "And drive an eighteen-wheeler."

After the chortling died down, one of his listeners said, "So." Then he questioned, "You plan to get some land and raise cattle?"

With his honest face still serious, Tom replied, "No, sir. I thought to rent her and the truck out to the others who might need their cattle shipped."

That got some knee and shoulder slaps and deep *har-har-hars*.

And one of the men called to her daddy, "Hey, Brice, you ever train that gal proper?"

Brice replied easily, "Her mother spoiled her rotten. I feel real sorry for any man that'd try to keep a steadying hand on that one."

There was another easy laugh.

When the right time came, Tom put in smoothly, "Browns have been known, for generations, to train and school recalcitrant creatures." He paused tellingly, "And females especially."

So the grizzled one questioned, "That right?"

Tom sighed with the admitted burden. "We've always accepted challenges."

After that laugh settled down, Miss Priss said, "The McCrea women are in the same category. We tame males."

That got challenging hoots.

But just then Garth Pippins drove his car down the lane. As they all watched in anticipation, he wheeled it into a slot by the other cars and stopped. That silenced the bunch of soot- and sweat-tacky loafers with their attentions riveted.

Here came the man that a woman had abandoned just yesterday. Another man was seriously teasing the woman . . . right there in front of most of the county residents. And each mind speculated on what would happen, whose side who would take if there'd be a fight.

That Garth could be tempered and sudden.

Tom wondered if Garth would actually leave his car out there—all alone—in the parking area. There were already all those pickup trucks at various angles along there.

Almost instantly, those people already in the yard realized Susan Lee had disappeared into the house. Was that deliberate? Tom eased down to a sprawl among the men.

Another young woman, Melody Commins, stood up and walked along toward where Garth would emerge from his car. A couple of the men rose from where they'd lounged. Was that because they were friends of Garth and intended to back him if Garth was in a temper? Or did they just want to see better if anything happened?

Tom speculated on whether or not Garth would attack him. He slid glances around his immediate area. Knowing the people would back off, he couldn't find anything that would hamper a fight. There weren't any tables or chairs.

Most of the men were resting on the chigger-free carpet grass. It was a yard that hadn't yet been invaded by the fire ants, so a body was safe lounging on that kind of grass.

If Garth wasn't too quick in his attack, it would be interesting to watch those lounging figures get out of the way.

Tom had already decided that Susan Lee wasn't in love with Garth, although even if she was, Tom would still have been a contender. And right then, he knew his try for her would have been very earnest, right up to the point she'd've tried to marry Garth.

To give him heart, he remembered the kisses she'd allowed him, her reaction to defending him against an improbable cougar's appearance, plus her slipup that their daughters would have the same surveillance her own mother gave to her.

A man strived for what he wanted. One way or another. It was so, even in this supposedly civilized time. And Tom thought of himself howling at the moon. If he actually felt that primitive, then Garth was carrying trouble in his pocket.

The first to greet Garth was Susan Lee's father. He said something that startled Garth. The avid watchers saw that was so. There was an intense exchange, and Brice even gestured as if telling Garth to leave. Garth put palm-down hands in front of his chest and apparently calmed Brice.

Tom figured it out. Garth was backing down. Brice had probably told Garth that Tom was there and he didn't want any problems between the two men.

Garth had agreed.

Tom found he was a little disappointed. If they'd fought, whether Tom won or lost, the reaction would be in his favor. Or would it?

Geo stood up.

Tom saw that. He hadn't known Geo was there. Susan Lee had affected his visual scan of people. He'd only needed to know where she was in that crowd. He'd been aware only of her. He was that zonked? And his eyes narrowed.

When Tom saw that Garth was neatly clean, he relaxed quite a bit. Garth hadn't been there for the fire Janella McCrea had set in the adjacent field. Garth hadn't shown up. Just about everybody else was there. It would be interesting to them all as to why Garth hadn't helped.

Tom noted their enclosed conversation as Garth Pippins and Brice McCrea walked toward the group which was waiting avidly for them. The curtain was about to rise. Tom's humor was touched. Felicia would love this whole episode.

Geo had almost invisibly moved closer to Tom. Tom was so touched. For Geo to take the part of a stranger—against a neighbor—was above and beyond the call for a temporary landlord.

Tom rolled over and braced himself up on one elbow so that he could look up at Geo. His soft voice had a very limited range as he told Geo, "Not this time."

Geo glanced down at his boarder and lifted his gaze back to Garth. Geo dismissed the direction given by Tom. Geo would do whatever he chose. How typically Geo Peterson was acting—a boneheaded man.

By then, Melody was closer to Garth and handed him a cold beer. She spoke to Garth, who glanced at her briefly, but he was concentrated on Brice, the father of his interest.

Then another car came from the lane and parked near those three. Geo commented to Tom, "Garth's parents are here." He waited a minute, watching, before he added, "And so's Garth's brother."

Then Geo's glance came down to Tom's as he asked softly, "Still a loner?"

And Tom laughed chuffs.

Another man, close by, felt the need to comment, "This could get real interesting."

Susan Lee didn't come outside to greet the newcomers. People around asked the approaching Pippins family, "Where you all been? We had to do your share, too."

Garth's father replied, "One little old brush fire and you couldn't handle it by yourselfs?"

There was the reply that was smug, "We did."

Mr. Pippins inquired, "How'd it start?"

Brice defended his wife, "Nobody knows."

Clyde put in, "It's under observation."

Garth's mother added to that, "I only had cookies, so I waited for Billy and Garth to get back. I tried to bake a decent cake."

Some droll male said, "Looks like another genius doing. You're a miracle cook, Lucinda."

She denied that.

"Where'd you and Billy go, Garth?"

Billy Pippins replied, "We was down that far hollow? There's a bunch of wild pigs down yonder. We need to set up a hunt."

Garth looked dismissively at Tom and asked, "You ever hunt wild pig?"

It was a gauntlet question. Tom recognized that. "I only carry a rifle and howl at the moon. I don't hunt."

"That figures." Garth dismissed Tom as a nothing excuse of a man.

Gently, but with sparkling lights in his shaded eyes, Geo asked, "What'd you do when you found the pigs?"

Garth's brother Billy replied, "We made it back to the truck bed in the nick of time."

Everybody there laughed. Not Garth. He turned a little red.

Someone else said, "Nothing tests a man's ability to run—flat out—like a wild pig."

Another commented, "It takes some doing to stop a wild boar. It is a challenge."

Garth asked Tom, "Wanna go try?"

Tom laughed. "I'm doing well to just work on a stray dog."

Garth gave a disrespectful snort.

Tom wondered if that was how Susan Lee had learned to snort. She had to break that habit.

Billy asked, "That dog a big yellow?"

Tom replied, "Yeah, you seen him?"

"We've tried a time or two to trap him. Garth wanted him. But he's smarter than us."

That's when Tom figured the Pippinses were real people, and Garth was just some sort of throwback.

Billy asked, "Where'd you see him?"

Tom evaded a reply. He didn't want the yellow trapped by anyone, including himself. He wanted the dog to agree to come with him. His reply to Billy was vague, "I don't know the countryside well enough to pinpoint him. I was taking pictures in a gully, and he watched me."

Garth asked, "Pictures?"

"I'm a photographer."

Garth's "Oh," negated that indulgence.

Geo put in, "You need to see the one he did of Dancer." That was Geo's chancy horse. The horse was so damned independent that a man had to convince him, every time, that he should agree to do as the man wanted. His name saluted the footwork that could unseat a man anytime, at all, if the man wasn't real alert. Mim's distaste for the animal was no surprise. She preferred Geo intact.

Everybody around that area knew about Dancer because he wouldn't allow any other horse to outdistance him. He was that competitive.

Garth asked, "What would Dancer do if a wild pig was after you?"

Geo was so easy and lax that his reply seemed mild. "He does as I say."

With some drollness, Mim asked, "Who doesn't?" She was nursing their new baby, with a flannel cloth making her modest.

Giving Mim a narrow-eyed look, Geo asked her, "When have you ever minded me?"

In the crowd's laughter over Geo's questioning, Mim tilted her head back and looked at the branches. "I'll think on that and let you know. I know I did once."

The crowd all loved the exchange. Geo was such a domineering man and such a nonconformist that Mim's sass was a delight.

Those around laughed. Under that sound Tom said to Geo, "You'll have to give me lessons."

And quietly, just to Tom, Geo replied, "That's like an egg-sucking hound asking to learn egg sucking."

"Now how'd I ever give you that impression?"

Geo replied in the lessening sound of exchanges in the crowd, "I've been around you long enough to form an opinion. Your momma taught you manners, so your real character is shadowed. I'd bet your daddy is a hard-nosed man."

"He was career navy." Tom considered Geo.

Geo nodded sagely. "That explains a lot."

"Now, how can just that information make me into an egg-sucking hound?"

"No. Not that," Geo countered. "Just one that knows all the angles."

"You think I'm smart? Streetwise? A new, wet-eared Texas boy from the town of Temple, Ohio?"

"Your daddy taught you to recognize just about any situation, and it was very telling when you declined to put a sedative in the dog's food."

"You tested me."

"Yep."

Tom folded his arms on his chest and smiled just a tad. He nodded a couple of times.

Geo asked, "When did you decide on me?"

"When it irritated the bloody hell out of you as I took your picture, but you endured me."

"Yeah." Geo had to agree.

"You're one of the few who endures irritation."

"What does Salty do about your picture taking?"

Tom grinned. "He's a ham."

Geo laughed out loud.

There were now listeners. Geo always had listeners. One asked, "Who's a ham?"

Tom was tolerant. "My dad. He loves to have his picture taken. He generally includes some of the littler kids. He explains that makes him look younger than he is."

"What's he do?" asked a questioner.

Tom shrugged. He deliberately neglected to mention Salty's car dealership. "He's navy and retired. He cooks and allows my mother to think her will is iron, but he rules."

More were listening. Mim said, "That sounds just like Geo. Don't let Salty come down here and be with Geo, I can barely control him now!"

Tom laughed first.

Geo was offended. When there was less laughter, he told his wife, "If I give you any more control over me, I'll have to get your excuse to leave a room."

"Yeah. I hadn't thought of getting that." She lifted their new little baby up to her shoulder and patted his back. She said to Geo, "From here on, you do that."

And meek voiced, Geo replied, "Yes'um."

The baby gave a really loud burp.

If they'd all been inside, the listeners' burst of laughter would have brought the house down around their ears. They were all very mellow. The exchange wasn't that funny. Tom was retaught that lifelong friends are very tolerant.

Susan Lee came out onto the porch, and Garth went her way as soon as she'd opened the door. To follow immediately would make Tom look unsure, so he stayed where he was. He even monitored the frequency of his casual glances to keep track of his woman.

As Tom looked the other way, Geo said, "She doesn't want to be with him."

"How do you know that?"

Geo explained, "She won't speak to him. He's begging."

"She hung up on him this morning after he told her she wasn't a lady."

Geo replied, "He's dead in the water."

Tom smiled a little. "How'd a man, clear out here in this dry country, find a saying like that?"

"My grandfather was a fisherman in the Gulf for a time during his formative years. His father was really mad at him and made him sign on for a year. It must have been an enlightening experience. He learned some really interesting words. And he could cuss in formal Spanish. It was beautiful, if you didn't know the meaning of the words. Grandmother didn't. Since he was always gentle, she thought he complimented her."

Tom considered Geo a while before he coaxed, "How'd you find that out?"

"I had friends who understood the words."

"That would help. I'll learn some Spanish cuss words."

"It just so happens, I can help you. It's Castilian Spanish, and quite beautiful. You have to speak it with a lisp, if you want to be authentic."

Tom smiled with humor and looked at Geo to share the idea of him lisping.

And just looking at Geo, Tom knew not even a lisp could flaw him. Tom told him, "I'm a quick learner."

"I have to ride fences tomorrow. You can go with me."

Be gone the entire next day? That made Tom give a very serious look up at the porch on which his love was ignoring that Pikkins person.

Geo soothed, "She needs some space. Leave her alone for a day and let her miss you."

Tom replied mildly, "If she shuns me after that, I'll take off one of your ears."

Geo chided, "I'm attached to my ears, and I might resist losing one."

"You could try."

Geo grinned with such humor.

Tom strolled over to Mim and asked her, "Would you mind if I took off one of Geo's ears?"

Did she say no? No. She asked, "Why?"

"I just wondered how you'd feel if I did."

She considered and replied with thoughtful kindness, "I'd probably slit your throat."

"Well, that's clear enough."

"Why would you lop off one of Geo's ears?"

"He advises me to allow Susan Lee a day free of my company so that she'll miss me. I'm not sure that's wise. That would give Garth a whole day to convince her she is attracted to him. She knows him better than she knows me."

Mim was logical. "She's known him for almost all her life. And if she can be lured away from him as easily as you lured her, then Geo might be right."

"It's too big a risk." Tom shook his head in doubt.

Mim was positive. "Geo knows everything. Do as he says."

So in order to give Susan Lee a good, solid remembrance of him, Tom went up on the porch and interrupted Garth's flow of words by saying, "We just about have time to make it. Sorry, Garth, we're committed."

Susan Lee frowned at Tom, and he wasn't sure she wouldn't snub him. He told her, "You look fine the way you are. He won't mind."

Garth questioned, "He?"

Tom supplied, "An old friend I've promised to visit. Susan Lee already knows him."

"Who is that?" Garth wanted to know.

With the clue from Tom, Susan Lee replied quite easily, "A blonde who lives beyond the ridge."

"What ridge? Who? I know everybody all around these parts. Who're you all going to see?"

Tom replied, "Why do you ask?"

"I'll go along."

"You aren't invited."

That shocked Garth, and he couldn't think of a response. It made him really angry, but there was nothing he could do about it. So he said to Susan Lee, "Stay here."

She was hostile. She replied, "Why should I do that?"

Garth instructed her, "You have guests. A lady stays with her guests."

"I was told—just this morning—that I'm not a lady."

She had Garth. So of course, Tom asked, "Who would ever say anything like that to you?"

She looked at Tom. "A cretin."

"No question about that."

Garth huffed, "Now, Susan Lee—"

But she interrupted and told Tom, "I'll be right out. I have to tell Momma."

He smiled.

As she left the porch, Garth said, "You're asking for a lesson in manners."

"Is that so?" Tom raised his eyebrows. "Who's going to teach me manners?"

"I will."

And Tom was nasty enough to burst out laughing. He laughed so hard that he lay a hand on Garth's shoulder for support, and Garth shrugged it off with some indignation.

Brice McCrea came up on the porch and asked, "What's the joke."

There was no humor in Tom's eyes. "He wants to teach me manners."

Brice considered Garth. "You can't be that dumb."

And Garth protested, "Now, Mr. McCrea—"

"Run along." Mr. McCrea then turned to Tom. "Come in and let me show you what I got today."

So Tom went inside the house with Mr. McCrea. Inside, Tom said, "I wasn't going to hit him."

Brice said, "I was afraid he'd try to hit you and you wouldn't have the choice."

"I don't have to hit back."

Brice cast a probing look at Tom. "Are you that much of a man?"

"I have a remarkable father."

"I'd like to meet him."

"He's been down over west of here visiting at Sam Fuller's place."

Brice nodded once to acknowledge Tom's information; then he said seriously, "You pay attention and don't fool around with my daughter unless you mean it. I won't have her hurt."

"I promise."

"Who's this blonde you're taking her to see?"

"A stray dog I found that's scared of people. He won't allow me close. I've been feeding him and leaving him water. There were cougar prints out there."

"Take care of Susan Lee."

"She doesn't get out of the car, and she'll have the rifle."

"You can trust her, she'd be good backup. She can handle guns." He studied Tom for a minute. Then he narrowed his eyes as he said, "You be careful."

Tom understood the wider ramifications of that caution. He replied, "Yes, sir."

Seven

Since Tom had replenished the dog's supply of food and water so recently, there had been no real reason for them to go there again. Tom had simply wanted to get Susan Lee away from Garth. How could anyone with a good, macho name like Garth be such a loser?

As they drove along, neither chatted. Susan Lee had her window open and the breeze was delighted to touch her, to play in her hair and to press her clothing against her. Tom wanted to do all that.

His glances were often on her. Almost as much as they were on where he was driving. She was a menace to safety. His. Not the car's.

Could it be real? Was this just sex? Just? What a diminishing word for something so powerful. He looked over at the silent Susan Lee, who wasn't doing anything to attract his attention—and she riveted him. She was alive and female, and he was intensely aware of that fact.

Had he ever been this possessive of a woman? Any female? He'd assuredly been interested, several times, but...possessive? Susan Lee McCrea was his. She belonged to him. Would she hold still for that?

She'd left her family and come along with him without any protest at all. Maybe she was just angry with Garth and wanted to punish him?

He looked at her again. She was too relaxed. He asked, "What are you thinking?"

"Momma set that fire to cover for you. What did you promise her?"

He smiled at the road coming toward them. He assured her, "Not our firstborn."

Her mouth was pulled down by the extent of her patience, and she said, "T-o-oommm."

"Well, she pushed. She wanted us here every Christmas, and I bargained it being just every other year."

"How can you commit me to such a farce?"

He was surprised. "Don't you want to come home for Christmas at all?"

She became impatient with him and waved her hands around as she asked, "Who says I'm going off with you, for Pete's sake?"

"Who's this Pete?"

She turned her head on the back rest to look his way. "Don't pull that on me. You are always putting in strings to lure me away from a subject."

He was surprised, "I do that?"

"Your mind works on too many levels at a time. You're hell to argue with because you're always distracted, and worse, you distract me!"

"I'll try to reform."

"You never will. You're just saying that to get past this criticism."

He gasped, "You're criticizing *me?*"

"See? It's just like you to say that. It starts a whole new angle, and you love it. You're avoiding replying to why you committed me to visiting your Yankee family, clear up there at the top of this country, in the middle of winter every other year."

He placated, "We'll renegotiate."

"You have not asked me to be a permanent fixture in your life."

He licked his lips and tilted his head at a new angle as he looked off into the mesquite-filled countryside and at the road coming toward them. He said, "Just a fixture?"

From the corner of his eye, he saw that she was regarding him. He considered her wordage. "Fixture? I had something a little more active in mind. However, I've got to get this snorting out of your system. Garth snorts. You probably got it from him."

"I do not snort."

"You've done it three times, just with me!"

She snorted.

He exclaimed, "There! See?"

"I was just showing you it is deliberate and therefore controllable."

"You've got flaws. Goodness to gracious! Who would ever believe somebody that looks like you could be a snorter? You're flawed! You caught it from Garth. He snorts." He threw that fault back into her lap.

"I am not at all, in any way like Garth." She was a tad strident.

"You sure look different. I'll give you that much."

"He's male."

Back to watching the road, Tom bobbed his head in several nods as he mentioned, "I *had* noticed you being female."

"He may snort because he thinks you're trifling with me."

"I've been trying," he admitted.

"How can you speak that way to a woman who is not as experienced as you?"

"I'm part of her education?"

She scoffed. "You wish."

"That isn't a very good tone for an inexperienced lady."

"Just this morning, Garth said that I'm no lady."

Tom shook his head in a serious way. "I can't stand up for a man that stupid."

"So, we'll follow that strand of diversion. You ordinarily stand up for men? You take their side?"

"'Course."

"Why?"

"Because males are about like beeves. We're taking a whole lot of derisiveness and criticism of our basic good."

She bubbled laughter.

He chided, "Now you know, being from around here, how important it is to sell beeves for something besides their hides. Men are the same way."

"What parts of you are—I don't believe I should ask."

He encouraged her. "Go ahead! Nobody learns much of anything if they don't ask."

"I pass."

He tilted his head back and watched the road from under his Stetson brim. "Ah. So. You pass the opportunity to respond. You play cards?"

"Ineptly. Do you?"

"Brilliantly. You can't be one of those under Felicia and not play. It was a rule."

"She loves it that much?"

"It kept us occupied in the bad weather."

"Oh, yes. That's right. I forget. You all have terrible weather up yonder."

"It's more interesting than what you get down in these here parts. It makes life more interesting to inquire about the weather and find out how people weathered the weather—"

She chided, "You used those words deliberately."

"Yep. Down here what do you have? Another nice day. It could get very dull and ordinary."

She protested, "But we appreciate the rain when it comes."

"Who did the rain dance in '92? You got overkill that year."

She agreed. "Our cisterns are still full."

He slid a glance over at his perfect guest. "You gonna give in today?"

"I heard you tell my daddy that you were going to behave yourself."

"What big ears you have!" he chided.

"It comes in handy."

He reorganized his query. "If I find I can't behave, are you going to give in?"

"Not yet."

His foot came off the accelerator as he bent over as if he'd been hit in his stomach.

She was alarmed. "What happened? What hit you?"

He groaned in a choked voice, "You did—with that 'not yet' you just flanged at me. You ought not do that to a man driving a car down a treacherous road like—"

"This is a perfectly normal road." She gestured with one hand, indicating the expanse of the road.

"I'll have to take you up to Ohio so you can compare. This is a ratty track at the most kind evaluation."

"We don't have the weather you all have up yonder. There's no need, here, for the elaborate roads you need up north."

He mentioned, "You're getting off the subject."

"What was that?"

"That you're going to give in to me, but 'not yet.' When?"

"I'll have to see."

"See." He tasted that word cautiously. "See... what?"

"If I want to."

"Honey." He sighed hugely, settled back and put his foot back on the accelerator. He glanced over at her for impact before he continued, "Coaxing you is just like coaxing that damned dog. You both know you're gonna give in. Why don't you? You'd save me a whole lot of time, not to mention the frustration."

Huffily she snapped back, "You're comparing me to a dog?" She breathed quickly and high in her chest. "So you think I'm a bitch?"

Her hostility was a tad high. He laughed.

She snorted.

He jerked around to look out his side window to conceal his hilarity. He moved forty-five different ways, trying to think of anything he could say that might soothe her, and he came up with, "No, I am so attracted to you that I can't believe you could be indifferent to me. You know I'm serious. I don't want you just for the wanting to be soothed. I want you even if you do snort. It'll be an irritation, but I can handle one flaw."

"I'm . . . flawed?"

"What went on at the pond that you were shocked someone had taken pictures there?"

She was prissy and her mouth was tight. "It is none of your business."

"But you have to realize how curious you make me about the pond. And why you were shocked over the idea that some pictures had been taken. What scarlet experience clouds your clear conscience?"

"Nothing."

"The very way you snap out that word shows a deep guilt." He turned his head once at the very idea. "You went parading around without any clothes? You went skinny-dipping?"

Her head snapped around as she asked, "Who—"

"Ah-hah! Who all was there?"

"No one." She was sitting stiffly, her head not on the back of the seat, and she was deliberately looking out at the passing countryside.

He gave a big, free sigh. Then he had the gall to say, "I'm glad I've been pure and don't have anything lurking in my conscience."

Through her teeth, she retorted, "There is nothing on my conscience!"

"I'm glad to hear you believe that. You may be a scarlet woman, but you feel it's normal."

"Tom!" she warned.

And again he laughed, so amused.

She said, "I believe I should go back to my house. Please take me there."

"Okay. I just have to replenish the dog's water. And if you don't mind, I will need you for backup again. Billy Pippins said they'd seen some wild pigs and just barely got onto the truck bed in the nick of time."

She exclaimed, "Wild pigs? They're a terror."

"Yeah. So while I'm replenishing the water, keep your eyes pealed and the safety off on the rifle. I'd appreciate it."

"Yes. I can do that. But, Tom, they're hard to kill. I've heard of men's thighs being gored in an attack by the boars. I know of a woman who lost a hunk out of her leg. They're very dangerous. Put the water pan closer to the road."

"You don't want me hurt?"

She wasn't about to tell him she was concerned for him. She said, "You'll have a better chance getting back to the car."

"I can't move the hubcap." He shook his head and frowned at the road. Then he glanced over at her and explained, "The dog's used to it being there. He could think I was being foxy, moving his dish toward the road, and he might understand I'm trying to get him, too, and he could vanish."

"Get him . . . too?"

"Now, buttercup, I've already told you a couple of times that I'm gonna get you. You know that for a fact."

She was snooty. "No way."

"All's I have to do is give you a killer kiss, and you're putty." He turned, and his brim didn't hide his eyes entirely.

She was big eyed, but she said a credible "Hah!"

He pulled over to the side of the road and rolled to a stop.

She gasped audibly and said, "Tom Brown, you leave me be."

He looked at her with innocent surprise. "Why, honey, we're here. I just told you about that."

She struggled to figure out the door's exit lock. "You're not going to touch me or give me any of your... killer kisses. I won't allow you to do that!"

"Okay. I won't. But you promised to back me."

She looked around. "Oh."

He watched her with close concern for her alarm. As innocent looking as she was, she would have to feel guilty. He said gently, "Yeah. This is where the dog is."

"I thought—"

He chided with all the virtue of a real seducer, "Now, how could you think I'd do a thing like that? Didn't I promise your daddy I'd behave?"

She looked at him as one looks at a snake that can smile. He was so serious and concerned. He was dangerous.

He asked gently, "You gonna back me?"

She was sure that he meant right then, watching, with the rifle ready for danger to him. But he could mean something else entirely. She regarded him seriously but didn't reply.

He got the rifle from the back seat and offered it to her.

She took it solemnly.

He said, "The safety's on."

She checked it, handling the weapon with knowledgeable skill. She took up her position, on the console, and clicked off the safety. She said, "Be careful."

He replied, "Put the ignition keys in your pocket. If someone came along, I wouldn't want those to be too convenient."

"Yes." She did that.

He told her, "When I come back to the car, I'm gonna kiss you very thoroughly."

She gave him a glance that didn't indicate any approval of such conduct. She said, "Watch in front of you and to the sides, I'll watch your back."

He replied, "Look around out here, too. And watch your own back."

"Yes. And listen. The wild pigs squeal and grunt."

"I do know about pigs."

"Be careful, Tom."

"It really isn't that dangerous. I'm just keeping you from being bored."

"If it's safe, why am I staying in the car?"

His look was serious. "Because you're too precious for me to risk until I'm sure about that cougar."

"And the boar."

"I don't believe this is the area where Billy and his sissy brother found the pigs."

She almost smiled. "You've led me to believe you're in real danger here, trying to care for that abandoned dog that's gone back to nature."

"A man does as he must."

"You admit it!"

"No. I was just commenting on having to keep this dog watered so's he can live."

"You keep flip-flopping so I don't know when to believe you're serious."

"I'm serious about this damned dog. And—" his head swung slowly around until he pinned her with his look "—I'm serious about you."

Before she could stop herself, she sassed, "In that order?"

"You want some proof?"

But she became cautious. She said, "You're going to help me enormously with my thesis."

He laughed so low in his throat that goose bumps went all over her, inside and out.

He settled his Stetson as if he'd done that all his life, and he looked around carefully, moving his head and looking at everything. Then he took up the bottle of water and moved into the break in the brush.

Susan Lee could see where the hubcap had been, but she didn't stare at Tom. She glanced all around him. She turned her head and monitored the road.

As she watched, she became aware of a movement along the ridge. Her attention was riveted. There was something there. She moved to the window. What if she called out? They had no signal. With her eyes darting around and going back to where she thought she'd seen something move, she softly whistled two trills.

Peripherally, she saw that Tom had stopped and frozen there. He did not move. How could she signal where he should look? She didn't need to find another signal, he was looking around very carefully. She eased from the car as soundlessly as she could and stood on the ground with the door in front of her.

Moving without being sudden, Tom filled the hubcap quietly. Then he looked around slowly, moving minutely, especially regarding the ridge, and he listened.

So did she. She held the gun at her shoulder and breathed in a calm rhythm. She was starkly alert.

Tom began to back toward her. He trusted his back to her.

Her eyes were never still as she monitored the range of vision.

A car came by and slowed. She didn't turn.

It slowed more, then turned and came quietly back, easing along as it silently rolled to a stop in back of Tom's car.

She didn't look.

Tom continued to back closer, being careful where he put his feet, watching his balance.

The other car's door opened so silently. A male voice whispered without sibilant sounds, "I'm here. Which direction?"

She tilted her chin toward the ridge.

He said, "I have a gun. Tell me when."

She whispered to the stranger, "I don't know."

There was silence. No birds, nothing.

Tom came past his handkerchief signal and stood, looking. Nothing moved.

He turned and came across the slight dip beside the road, and he smiled past Susan Lee. Softly, softly, he almost just mouthed the words, "Well, Tweed—"

Equally quiet, Tweed replied, "Is she getting set to shoot you?"

Hushed, Tom explained, "Naw. She saw something up on the ridge. We're a little spooked because there've been cougar tracks along here." Then he grinned at his unrelated brother. "How are you, Tweed? How'd you happen along?"

"I heard there was a brush fire over here, and I just wondered if the citizens were burning you at the stake."

Tom opened his back door and told them, "Get in." He said that to include both of them. They entered the car, and in the back, both men heard as Susan Lee put the safety back in place. Tweed didn't do that with his gun. He was still looking around. "Any idea what it was? Uh, you haven't introduced me."

"I was avoiding claiming you. Susan Lee, this here's one of my brothers?" That was a do-you-understand questioning statement. "He lived with the Browns for a while, and we had a hard time finding him again. His name's Tweed. He'll tell you how come he took that name sometime, when he's had a couple of beers."

Susan Lee glanced over and smiled, but she was still looking.

"What'd you see?" Tom asked her.

"It was either the dog or the cougar. We didn't have a signal."

Tom assured her, "You did perfectly."

She explained, "That's one of the family's signals. One sharp, shrill whistle means to get back right now. Two soft ones mean to watch out."

Tom nodded. "Good."

"I wasn't sure you could hear me."

Tom replied, "It was really quiet until some yahoo came roaring down the track in a jalopy."

"Don't call that magnificent machine a jalopy. I'm very fond of that vintage vehicle."

Tom mentioned, "I'm just surprised it runs." Then he put a hand on Tweed's shoulder. "I'm a godfather."

"Who did that out of a clear blue sky?"

"The Petersons. They had a new little boy and named him for me."

Tweed shook his head. "That's 'cause they don't know you very well. Just think of saddling a kid with a godfather like you. Well, maybe you won't be around long. That way, you won't ruin him."

Susan asked quietly, "Ruin him?"

Tom said to Tweed, "Now look what you've done."

"He's a terrible man." Tweed said that earnestly. "Some day when you're braced for it, I'll tell you why he's no longer living in Ohio."

"And I've called you *brother?*"

"He gave our brother Bob purple condoms on his wedding night! That's a clue right there."

"Well, Bob had hustled Jo so that I thought she ought to have time to reconsider before she was caught."

Tweed asked Susan Lee, "Are you old enough for this conversation?"

Tom protested in a soft voice, "You're the one who brought up the purple condoms."

"No, it was you. You took them right up to the attic. I remember hearing that very clearly."

Susan Lee inquired in a hushed voice, "Attic?"

Tom quietly confirmed it. "Yeah. There's some kind of peculiar gene in our family that gives us an affinity for attics. Cray and his wife lived in one for almost a year. Bob and Jo are still in the one at home."

"Haven't they ever come out of it?"

"Oh, yes. Especially when they have kids. Bob does take Jo to the hospital for that sort of thing."

Tweed smothered his laughter. "I've missed so much of you strange Browns. But I lived with you long enough that nothing you all do surprises me."

Susan Lee snitched in a whisper, "Tom's trying to tame a dog that's chancy."

Tweed did inquire, "Now, why are you doing that?"

Tom shrugged. "He looks like a good animal."

Tweed asked softly, "What would you do with a dog? You're never anywhere for very long. He'd get used to you, and then you'd move on."

Susan heard. She looked at Tom very seriously. "Tom's a tramp?" she asked Tweed.

Tweed laughed soft chuffs and said to Tom, "Just think of all the answers I could give her for you. But Susan Lee, I'll tell you the truth. Tom's a good man."

She gave Tweed a side-eyed look and replied, "You're kin."

"Not actually. They just claim me because I lived with them for a couple of years."

She smiled.

Tweed said, "I haven't seen a thing since I got here. I have a couple of rifles in the trunk of my chariot, want to take a look around?"

"If it was the dog, I don't want to go tramping around carrying a gun. It might spook him."

"What kind of dog is he?"

"Probably some mix, but he's like a Great Dane crossed with a boxer. Something had cut him right back here, and the blood was like tar when I saw him."

"How long ago was that?"

"A couple of times in this last week."

Tweed considered that and said, "He must have a reason."

Tom replied, "I've looked around for a wreck or where a wreck happened, but I can't find anything." Then he considered Tweed. "The brush fire's out, want to come back to Petersons' with us?"

Susan Lee put in, "I probably should go on back home."

Tom smiled at her as he said, "Not right away." Then he asked Tweed, "Can you come along?"

"Since they aren't trying to burn you at the stake, I should go back to our place. I was looking for that damned bull, Hugo."

Tom laughed. He told Susan Lee, "Tweed spends most of his time trying to coax that bull to behave."

"No, we just don't want somebody else sending him to the butcher's. If anyone sells him, it has to be us."

Susan Lee asked, "What's he look like?"

Tom volunteered, "I have a picture of him back at the Petersons'."

And Susan Lee told them, "Once, long ago here in TEXAS, there was a terrible murder that was covered up. So in protest, people painted 'murder' on the side of a steer. It was allowed to roam free to protest the fact that murder had been done."

Tweed nodded. "I'd heard of that. Nobody took the steer or killed it. It went where it wanted to go."

Susan Lee said, "There are a lot of old stories anyplace you go. We have our share. Probably one of the best brags was the TEXAS Rangers. A town had called the Rangers for help because there were two sides fighting in a town and people were being killed. So the Rangers sent help . . . on a train!

"There were people at the station, and one man got off. He was a Ranger. The people were shocked and protested that there was only one Ranger. And the Ranger replied logically, 'There's only one fight.'"

Tom put in, "We have strange people up north, too, and—"

Susan Lee sassed, "It's the weather that makes the Yankees strange. Here in this glorious state, strange behavior is looked on as being eccentric."

The two Browns looked at each other and smiled.

Tom tried again, "Come along to Petersons'. I've talked about you, and they'd be pleased to meet you."

"I will another time. I have to get on back. If you see a humongous, cantankerous bull, ask his name. If he says 'Hugo,' corral him and we'll come a-running."

"I'm not going out looking for a cantankerous bull. I'm many things, but I'm not stupid."

Tweed complained, "That bull's stealing our cows."

"That is a shame." Tom was unfeeling.

"What would he do to a wild boar?" Susan Lee was curious.

"He's so smart, he'd avoid the confrontation."

Tom sympathized, "It must be demeaning to admit you're not as smart as a bull."

"How'd you know that?" Tweed asked.

"You're looking for him. It seems to me, you were looking for him when you found Connie."

"Yeah." Tweed looked off, remembering.

Tom said in a low voice, "I didn't mean to rake that up."

"You didn't. It was a miracle to find her. She could have died out there."

"She was lucky." Tom was so serious.

He was so serious that Susan Lee wouldn't touch a question at that time, and she was silent, watching the two men.

Tweed roused himself and put a hand on Tom's shoulder. "Behave. I'll come over another time. Give my regards to the Petersons and congratulate them on their new little boy."

Tom smiled. "I'll do that."

Then Tweed said, "Susan Lee, you have to come over and visit Connie. And you have to see the paintings that Mrs. Fuller did."

"Thank you. I'd love to."

Tweed said, "Us Browns are getting a whole section of us down in these here parts. You can look us over and see if we're acclimating enough."

She laughed silently.

Then Tom whispered, "Look."

Eight

Since Tom was pointing back into the brush, both of the other occupants of his car looked in that direction.

The big yellow dog was coming down the incline in full sight. He stopped and looked around, listening and observing. He gave the two cars careful study; then he went to the filled hubcap to lap at the replenished water. He lapped, then raised his head to look around and listen before he lapped again.

Softly, Tom said, "He's careful."

Tweed added quietly, "He's becoming wild, just like Hugo."

"You mean the dog'll gather a pack?"

"Yeah." Tweed replied thoughtfully, "Dogs allow inferior males to join a pack. Hugo won't do that in his herd. He wants all the cows for himself."

Tom said musingly, "I've never heard of a domesticated dog that could live off the land. They don't know how to kill game well, so they cripple creatures. Killing is a learned skill. Domesticated dogs don't go wild and stay healthy. I need to get this dog back to civilization."

"I wonder why he's so spooked."

"Just today, I heard of a couple of guys who've tried to trap him."

Tweed breathed the sound, "Ahh. Clumsy."

"Seems so."

Susan Lee had been listening to them. "Was that the Pippinses?"

Tom looked at her before he confirmed it. "Yeah." She didn't reply.

Tweed stayed with them as they observed the escapee. The dog checked out the area, left his mark here and there and sniffed around. He came back to the hubcap, lapped some more water, then flopped down and rested.

After a time, Tweed said, "I've got to be getting back. Great to see you two. Come see us."

The couple got out with him and stood talking a while, then waved Tweed off.

Standing there, Tom put his arm around Susan Lee. "I love you, you hussy."

"I'm no hussy."

"What were you doing out at the pond?"

"It's none of your business."

"Well, if I plan on being serious about you, I have to know the scandals you've been involved with so that I can appear to be aware about that side of you. I can't go jumping into such a committed tangle without knowing. What did you do out at the pond?"

"Nothing to embarrass you."

"How about you?" Tom asked. "Why do you blush and object to talking about it?" He licked his smile. "Are you a scandal for the whispering old ladies?"

"No."

"How come we're talking about that when you didn't even acknowledge that I told you I love you? Do so many men declare their hearts to you that you are immune to surprise?"

"I don't believe you're serious. We hardly know each other."

He smiled down at her, his lashes just about covering his eyes. He said slyly, "We know each other almost enough. And I'm taken with you. Let's not stand out here, this exposed. I'm not entirely sure it was the dog up on that ridge. Let's get in the car and watch him a while. We can talk."

Only thing was, he didn't talk. He petted her and distracted her from watching the dog altogether.

He told her that he was attracted to her. That it was so bad for him that he felt like he was burning inside his body. He'd never felt that way about any other woman in all his days.

He said he could only think about her, and thinking of her kept him from all the other things he ought to be doing. People talked to him, and their voices just faded away as she came into his mind. He'd wonder what she was doing and who might be sweet-talking her.

No matter where he was, he thought about her. He dreamed of her. He yearned for her to be with him. Against him. His body hungered for hers and his hands wanted to hold her close to him. She was so soft.

Her mouth was so sweet to taste. Her lips drove him crazy. He couldn't get enough of her. His heart was hopelessly lost to her.

She managed to form the word slowly with her red-dened, kiss-swollen lips, "Baloney."

He lifted his head from her throat and asked in an injured tone, "How can you say a rude word like that when I've opened my heart to you?"

"You're...practiced."

"Talking?" He sounded indignant. "'Course I'm practiced talking, I've been doing it for twenty-six years!"

With effort, she clarified, "Loving."

"I wish." He was disgruntled. He rubbed his big hand hard on her soft stomach and around to her hip. "You wear too many clothes."

"Good thing."

He went on being critical. "And you're smart mouthed. You ought to be pliant and sweet to me."

"This part of my thesis will blaze on the paper. I'll probably have to use asbestos. Is there any left commercially?"

"No."

She sighed, and he watched her chest do that. She mourned, "I probably won't be able to find any kind of paper that can handle something that hot."

"Kiss me."

She almost shook her head. "You've already had today's share."

"How many?"

"Fifty."

In shock, he pulled his head back and objected, "I couldn't have gotten fifty kisses in this soon. You can't count. Besides snorting, you can't count! What kind of kids will we have! Snorting and not being able to even count!"

"You're hysterical."

"I thought only women were hysterical."

"*Men* say only women are." Then she added, "You know what? Your hysteria helps my thesis no end."

"If you use my hysteria in your paper, you have to tell why I'm hysterical because you're making me needy and suffering all kinds of pangs and rejections."

After a little silence, she inquired with some careful interest, "Has this approach ever worked before this?"

"I've never wanted a woman the way I need you."

"You said that too fast. You're practiced."

He frowned at her. "You asked me a question, and I gave you the answer. It's the truth. You're driving me crazy."

"Baloney."

"Feel what you're doing to me."

She wiggled to get loose as she said briskly, "I think I'll go up on that ridge and see what was there. There ought to be prints. If it's the cougar, I'll give you a holler."

"I'm not letting you out of this car."

She paused and enunciated carefully, "Whatever was up there will be easier to handle than you."

He was offended. "I've been a perfect gentleman!"

"Baloney."

He told the car's ceiling, "Snorting, unable to count and selfish. And she's taken with a word like baloney!"

"You're a sex maniac."

In exasperation, he told her, "I never was before this."

"Tweed said you were run out of Ohio. Women do that?"

"Their boyfriends."

"I can believe it. Garth may shoo you clear out of TEXAS."

"He can try." He shifted on the seat and gave her breathing room. "You're really something. You make me so hungry for you. Why you? Why a woman that snorts and can't count kisses and—"

"You tend to get in three or four at a time without breathing. You count it as one, while it's really a sneaky three or four. You pad the bill that way. You are a-way over the limit."

"I didn't know there was a limit."

"There is. I try to stop you so you won't hurt."

He looked over at her, his hair mussed, breathing through his partly opened mouth. "So you know I hurt."

"I don't want you to—"

"Good!" And he reached for her.

"No, no, no, no, *no!*"

Surprised, he argued, "But you just said—"

"Keep your distance!"

"You're a tease."

"How can you say that when I've resisted most of the way."

"Well . . . you breathe." He was earnest, imparting vital information. "You sit and look out the window, and when I talk to you, you smile at me."

"I shouldn't smile at you?"

"That soft smile says you like me."

"Liking you is wrong?" That did startle her.

He was positive. "No."

With slow words, she told him very clearly, "I haven't had to struggle this much with a male since I was fifteen. I believe you are a late bloomer. You should have learned control before now."

He slid his glance over at her and smiled just a little. "It would scare you spitless to know how much control I've been using."

"I'll drive me home. You stay here with that other wild dog."

She sat there—in control—but her hair was mussed, her lips were kiss softened and her eyelids were droopy. She watched him as if waiting for him to exit the car.

He reached over and pulled her close to him. He took the keys from her pocket. Then he got out of the car, walked around and got into the driver's seat. He started the car, looked over at her and smiled just enough so that her back shivered and her nipples peaked. Then he drove, easing onto the roadbed, moving along.

She watched him. First she'd watched a wild dog, now she was watching a man who was even more unpredictable.

She glanced at the landmarks. Along there were forked trees or a stump or a ruined barn with dry, air-parched, iron-hard boards. He was taking her home. She wasn't sure she wanted to go home right then. She tilted her head and allowed the wind to calm her.

Why did men think women weren't as affected as they? Why were women the ones who had to resist and protest and chide? Women's desires and needs were just as intense. She not only had to control him, but herself!

And she wondered what it would be like for a role reversal as she sought him out? Why was it always the woman who had to set the rules and limits? Well, that was easy enough to understand. Men couldn't get pregnant.

When had he changed direction? That rock was on the way to the Petersons'. What was he up to now? The Petersons were at the McCreas'. Did he think she was so stupid that she wasn't aware of that? She slid a glance over at him and studied him.

His whole attention was on the road. At least his eyes were in that direction. He was stern looking. He was beautiful.

His left arm was resting on the windowsill. His hair was being tousled by the wind. His Stetson was on the back seat. He'd tossed it back there when Tweed had left. Then Tom had hustled her into the cramped, limited passenger side of the front seat.

She realized that if he'd intended her to allow him her body, he'd have put her in the back seat with him after Tweed had left. She considered that was strange behavior for a determined man.

Yet he'd coaxed and scolded and been exasperated by her resistance. But he'd put her in an impossible place—for his alleged purposes—and had deliberately given her a choice. Either she would agree to make love and get into the back seat with him, or she would resist and stay where she was.

So while he had been very determined and coaxing, he'd been considerate enough to allow her free choice.

Interesting.

Her heart was soft. "Where are we going?"

He didn't look at her. "I'm kidnapping you."

"Oh?" She considered that. "How much are you asking from Daddy?"

"How much are you worth?"

She pondered, squinching her face and working her lips. "I don't think he has that much."

He slid an amused, wicked look at her. "Maybe the bank will lend him enough."

"While Daddy is partial to me, I do believe he'd shed crocodile tears and wring his hands as he suggested you keep me."

"Okay."

"He would insist on you making me a bona-fide wife."

"Oh."

She sighed with great patience. "Yes. He has a double-barreled shotgun that he got when I was born, for just such an occasion."

"Oh."

"That's a pretty weak 'Oh' from a man your size."

"I hadn't thought they'd miss you."

"You say that after Momma set that fire to cover for you?"

"Well, I just thought she wanted to get *rid* of you! I had no idea a'tall that she meant for us to marry. That makes this whole caper more serious."

"I've been indicating that all along."

He frowned over at her. Then he said in disgust, "You're a nuisance." He could say that because he'd been hearing those very words ever since he'd moved in with the Petersons. Such things tend to rub off on the listener.

She studied her hands rather elaborately, knowing that he glanced at her, and she said, "When we marry, I'll just love redecorating the house."

"Uh-oh."

Very sweetly she continued, "And I play bridge. There are three tables in the group?" That was an is-that-clear questioning statement. "So if someone can't make it, you'd have to substitute."

"My God."

She considered her hands admiringly. "You did say that you're an expert?"

Disgruntled, he admitted it, "Yeah."

She tilted her chin up to add, "And I wear curlers with picks to bed."

He put on the brakes, watched the nonexistent traffic very carefully and turned around with screeching brakes.

She laughed. She bubbled laughter. Her eyes spilled delight, and she couldn't not laugh.

He slammed on the brakes. In a flash he'd unbuckled his seat belt, reached over in quick, practiced dispatch, unbuckled hers and hauled her over the console as he pushed his seat back and slid his body under hers.

He kissed her outrageously.

He made a malleable mass of her cells and had to continually try to reshape them. She moaned and breathed brokenly as her lips moved and worked urgently to get more.

Then he put her back onto the passenger seat, rebuckled her belt and put himself back under the wheel with his own belt connected. Just like that. But he trembled. His hands, his hair. He was in iron control, but there were those little betraying clues as to his vulnerability.

He said, "I'll take all of that under advisement."

Was she zombied? No. She had to struggle to form the words, but she did manage, and she said, "How kind."

He turned around again and drove on toward the Petersons'.

She knew, full well, that the Petersons were over at her house with her parents and all the rest of the fire brigade, who were still recovering from putting out the McCreas' fire. Just what was Tom up to, taking her out to their place when no one else was around?

Well, Willy would be there. Tom had probably forgotten that. She sat silent, and smugly waited for him to be surprised by all the chaperons there'd be around at the Petersons'.

Tom drove along that long mesquite-crowded lane and came out of it onto reasonably cleared land and the parking places for company. There was not one soul anywhere in sight.

Her head turned and her eyes darted around and she became wary. She glanced over at her driver.

Tom smiled at her. His mussed-up hair and shaggy brows and tanned chin looked particularly arrogant. He felt he was in the catbird seat. That was obvious.

She raised her eyebrows and told him, "No, you're not."

"Not—what?"

"You're not going to get me."

"Why, Susan Lee McCrea! How primitive thinking you are. What *ever* is on your mind that you'd say those words to a fine young man like me?"

She wasn't swayed. She watched him with that rejecting look.

He stopped the car and turned off the engine. It was silent. So was the out-of-doors . . . silent. They were alone? How could they possibly be alone in a place like the Petersons'?

Tom said, "Want to see my darkroom in the shed? I'll show you the pictures I made of the dog. And those of you I haven't showed to the family."

A darkroom in the shed was not a bedroom. Maybe she could do that. "What pictures of me?" Then she thought of the pond and her face became still.

He smiled inside his chest. No woman could resist seeing pictures of herself. "At the barn dance."

That was okay. She could see those. She opened her door and got out of his car.

He had taken his Stetson from the back seat and was settling it on his head as he met her at the hood of the car, and they walked on around to the shed.

They went under a big oak that had been listed as being almost four hundred years old. It was called the Council Tree. No one knew why or who had met under it. The stories varied.

The lower limbs of the oak were shored up with slender columns of bricks. The limbs were so long and low, they'd rot if they were allowed to lie along on the ground. And Tom told Susan Lee about the porch that had been built into an old oak over at the ranch where Tweed lived.

"It isn't a deck," he explained. "It's a formal porch. You'll have to see it. Sam's wife, Ethel, had it built. It has a curved grand staircase. They used the porch for entertaining. They'd have a band on the ground and dance on the porch. It is really elegant."

Susan Lee agreed, "When Miz Fuller was living, my parents were guests there. We have Sam over on occasion, but he hasn't entertained in years. Not like he used to. We did go to Tweed's wedding."

"I was there! How come I didn't meet you then?"

"You were hassling that nurse."

"Oh."

"Yeah."

He grinned widely. "She was a flirt."

"You didn't mind."

And Tom laughed.

"Since I witnessed your conduct with her, I'm more careful for me."

He glanced at her as they walked along, and looked down at her as he smiled just a little. "You got her beat all hollow."

"You come up with more sweet talk. You're too smooth."

"I'm surely glad you think I'm smooth. I do try."

"A woman is a fool to listen to a smooth-talking man."

"I didn't know that. I thought women liked hearing nice things about themselves."

"You're too practiced."

"Well," he explained with candor, "my daddy was a sailor, and they are the best talkers in the world. Even though they do walk funny for a while after they land."

"See?" She gestured. "You have an answer for everything. I've never met a smoother man."

"You need to get up to Ohio. All the men in Ohio talk thisaway. Well, they may not use TEXAS words, but they are all smooth talkers. The only ones that can beat them are those guys in Indiana."

Then he added thoughtfully, imparting information, "The Chicago guys don't flatter a woman, they just give her the opportunity to know them. The guys on the West Coast talk another language, altogether, and unless a woman is from there, nobody knows if they're smooth or not because nobody understands them. And those on the East Coast don't realize there are people beyond New York's border."

"You've done a lot of research."

"Being a photographer opens a lot of doors." He smiled at his wordage as he opened the door to the shed.

She went inside. He was right on her heels and he closed the door.

She stopped and looked back at him. He indicated the direction, "Straight ahead. That cubicle in the corner is my darkroom."

As she maneuvered past tractors and machine parts, she said to Tom, "I'm impressed Geo allowed you to use this part of the shed. How'd you manage that?"

"I took a picture of him with Mim on his lap."

"He loves her."

"You're right. He tolerates everybody else, but he really loves Mim."

"Let me see the picture."

"He has the only copy. He made me destroy the negative."

So Susan Lee studied Tom for a minute and then asked suspiciously, "When he told you to do that, what did you do with the negative?"

"I destroyed one."

She tasted the word. "One."

"Yep."

"What will he do if he finds you have another?"

"He'll kill me."

"Yeah." She nodded thoughtfully as she looked around at walls covered with stark pictures of landscapes, animal prints, rocks, gullies and—her.

There were all sorts of pictures of Susan Lee Mc-Crea. At the barn dance, at the hospital with the new little Tommy Peterson, in the parking lot, talking—

"How'd you take those?"

"I have this miniature camera that fits in one hand and takes pictures from between my fingers."

"That's impossible."

He gestured at the pictures. "That's proof."

She studied the pictures of herself.

He silently watched her do that.

She finally said very seriously, "You make me look good. I'm not that good-looking."

He denied that. He gestured at the prints pinned on the wall before her. "That's the proof."

"Where are all the ones you had to throw away?"

He nodded as he resettled his Stetson. "I pitched the one with your eyes rolled back in your head, and the one where your tongue hung out of your mouth to one side, and the one—"

She hit his shoulder, and he laughed.

He took out his wallet from his hip pocket and opened it. "This is the one." He handed her the wallet.

It was she, sitting on the console, holding the rifle, looking down as she released the safety. The light was from outside, backlighting her and making her ethereally calm...and deadly. It was a remarkable contrast. It was brilliantly done.

He said in his throat, "That's you. You are that woman. I want you to back me."

That said it all. He would be the one taking the risks, but he wanted her backing. He wanted her there with him.

She asked, "How can you be that sure?"

"Look at the picture."

She did. "That's light and shadow. It's a chance photograph. In another light, you would see another woman. Another me."

"Another facet. You aren't one person. We are all facets of all our ancestors. You have this in your background. This is your genes. You are this woman when you need to be." His voice roughened. "And when I hold and kiss you, you are another woman."

"You've become entranced by a photograph."

"No. Look at the shadings of the woman I know." He gestured at the pictures of her he had pinned up on the walls.

"I'm not that good-looking or that charming." She was serious and spoke soberly. "You should have kept the ones with my eyes rolled back and my tongue hanging out."

"There weren't any like that."

She told him, "I'm not perfect."

"Neither am I."

"That picture isn't a real person. It's a flat image of a chance combination of hues, lights and shadows."

He added, "Based on your four-dimensional image."

"You're not taken with me. The image you 'see' is what you 'read' into the picture of me. You believe your imagination."

"Everything you say is correct. But you ignore that I know the original piece of humanity that made the picture, which is you."

"You spend too much time in a darkroom with your imagination, the filters, the waggling of your fingers under the developer to soften shadows. You've created a being from never-never land. I'm not she. I could only disappoint you."

If she had been sassy or flirtatiously inviting compliments, he could have believed her rejections of her image, but she was very serious. And it was probably then that he knew he would marry her. He would get past any obstacle. This was a woman to enrich his life and who could share his love of form and color.

He gazed on her and his eyes saw what they wanted. His soul saw her as she really was. It was the way any loved woman is viewed. He said, "I love you."

And she became impatient. "Bosh."

"At least you didn't snort."

"Thank you for showing me these versions of photographs." And being honest, she added, "I believe your stark ones are mostly static."

He was jolted. "The cougar prints over my boot prints?"

"That one is brilliant."

"But—"

She went down the line and pointed in a pistol manner, "This one, this, this, this and all those are dead in the water."

He exclaimed, "Geo said that!"

"He didn't like those pictures?"

"He said, 'Dead in the water,' just that way. Where do you all get that sailor wordage out here in the wilds of mesquite-covered West Texas?"

"All the men around here went to sea. It's a rule. Then they love any part of Texas they can find."

"Your granddaddy sent your daddy off to sea? All these Texans must be cantankerous."

"No, it was my great-grandfather who sent my grandfather off to sea to get him out of great-grandmother's hair for a year."

"What a recalcitrant bunch of people TEXANS must be, if their parents have to keep shipping them off to get rid of them for a while."

"It's similar to the Grand Tour the English did with their sons in olden times."

"Ahh. So that was the solution. My parents lived in such a little town that at eighteen we were all shipped off to colleges at some distance."

"There is more than one way to skin a cat."

"I have heard that." He moved his body a little as he shifted closer to her. His hands were innocently in his trouser pockets so that he didn't look grabby. He said, "I need a kiss."

"No."

He was shocked. "Why not?"

"This is a darkroom. I can't be friendly with you in such a spacious, secret place. It would be foolish."

"You kiss me in the car."

"But never in open spaces where I can't get away."

"You don't trust me."

She looked at him and smiled a little.

"That's an inviting smile."

"No, that's because you know I can't trust you, so you're trying to open up a debate, which you believe you will win." She went to the door and opened it. "I have to go home."

He didn't object. She hadn't said she wouldn't kiss him again, she just said she wouldn't in open places. He'd get her into the confined space of his car, and then he could kiss her.

So he did kiss her there in the front seat of his car, and the console was its usual nuisance.

She finally convinced him that no one would be left at the McCrea house, and she could go home. And she was right. There were only McCrea cars.

As he slowed his car to a stop, he told her, "You're going to have to get yourself into the house. Your daddy would only need one look at me, and you'd never get out of the house again. But, honey, you better get it settled in your mind. I'm gonna get you."

Nine

Susan Lee considered Tom's mussed hair, which he'd clawed back with tense fingers. She noted the fact that he couldn't breathe through his nose because he was still hyper from kissing her. While he tried to appear easy, he was tense and restless. He made slight movements because he was so strung up.

She told him, "You're a brilliant photographer. My parents will love this print of me."

"Your daddy will instantly realize that I want you."

She scoffed, "No."

"Yeah. It's so obvious that the camera loved you. He'll know it was me using the camera."

She studied him for a minute. "You're really strange. I'm not quite sure how to handle you and I—"

Fervently he promised, "I can teach you to handle me."

"I suppose that's salacious?"

"Yes."

She pinched her mouth in censure. "Somehow that isn't surprising."

"Let's go over into the Big Bend country and get lost for a couple of days."

"That is an interesting sounding invitation. I've heard so much about that area, but I must decline."

He accused, "You're a coward."

So using the questioning statement, she had to explain, "My parents would be so fascinated by the outing that they'd gather friends of their own? We'd find ourselves in a caravan of sightseers."

"In Big Bend park, we could lose them."

She questioned, "You've forgotten about helping your mother search out your sisters when they had male company?"

He shook his head in defeat. "Yeah."

"All males forget such things. They think they are the only ones who've ever sneaked around with a female and nobody would ever notice."

"You're discouraging me."

She put out her hands in a gesture of openness. "No, I'm dangling a tidbit that might tempt you into considering me for more than just a romp in the hay."

He was shocked. "You're plotting to land me?"

She agreed. "I'm considering you."

He sighed gustily and looked out of his car window. He had his left elbow on the driver's windowsill and his right hand was resting on his wrist over the top of the wheel. He looked at her over the top of his right arm in a discouraged way. "I think you ought to romp around with me and allow me a good review first. Then you can see if you'll snare me."

"Yeah. I'd do all the things you want, and would you stick around? You'd know what I'd be like. You'd know all my faults—"

He mentioned with a dramatic sigh, "Yeah, curlers with stick pins."

"That's turned you off?"

He was positive, "Considerably."

"Well, we could see how I'd be straight haired." Her hair was naturally wavy and ducktailed.

He studied her across the car's console. "I like all those little wisps."

Being the helpful type, she offered, "I could use a curling iron." She looked at him and lifted her brows in a rather asinine manner. "As you hear, I am willing to bend enough. What about you? What about substituting at my bridge club?"

"Maybe your mother would fill in. If she'd set a fire to keep me out of trouble so that I can court you, she might help you to trap *me!* She just might be willing to relieve me the section in your rules about substituting in a female bridge party. I can't just go around pulling down my girdle and exchanging gossip."

She corrected gently, "Women don't gossip. They exchange information."

"And scandals."

"Of course. That is an important point. Once we know the scandals, we can reshape our own lives so it doesn't happen to us, and that would give us our lesson for that month. Then, too, it could be possible to figure out a solution to the scandal that might help the participants."

He considered that. "You would help others with their problems?"

She explained kindly, "We're mostly called busy-bodies."

"Oh."

After a pregnant pause, she asked suspiciously, "What's that 'Oh,' mean?"

"I see."

She questioned, "See . . . what?"

"How you look at things. And let's just stop this line right here. I'm not going any further in this discussion and get my hair singed off with your resulting fury."

"I never say anything that could singe hair."

He agreed. "That's probably true, you'd do it with one look."

She gave him just such a look, and he put both hands to slapping at his hair putting out the "fire" that her look had set.

Susan Lee was patient. Several times she took in a deep breath through her mouth and released it through her nose in an extremely apparent manner that showed her to be an adult who can endure odd behavior.

He said, "I'd like to kiss you witless."

She was impatient. "By now, all the kids have joined my parents at the windows. This has somewhat less-ened the intentness of my parents, because they've been trying to keep the kids from brushing against the glass curtains and betraying the fact that they're all watch-ing."

"It must be tough to be the oldest girl in a family."

"All of it means I'm having to break the trails for those coming along. I have great sympathy for Eski-mos."

That gave him something to figure out, and he guessed, "The cold?" Even his tone doubted it.

She nodded. "Breaking trails."

He let it go. He invited, "Go with me tomorrow to refill the hubcap?"

"Thank you. I'd be delighted." She opened her door.

He stayed put. "About eight?"

She turned back and asked, "Eight? In the *morning?*"

"Yeah."

"It's Sunday. I have to go to church."

"Why?"

"Well, it's just something we do."

"When can you go with me?"

"Why don't you come for dinner, tomorrow noon, and we can go then."

"Dinner. A suit." He considered that very seriously. He gave her a weighing look, then said, "Okay." But he leaned forward and turned the ignition key.

She completed her car exit as he revved the motor in encouragement. She dallied and gave him "the look" over her shoulder, and he waved his hands around his head to ward off the scorching of his hair. She enunciated, "My father may well find you are unsuitable."

"I said I'd wear a suit!"

"Good grief." She finished her exit and slammed the car door as he went forward enough to curl the car out of the parking area and slide a little as he then got to their lane. He was showing off.

She took a steadying breath and was braced for comments as she went inside and was confronted by her father, who said, "He may be just a tad careless with our baby, a man that drives a car thataway."

She replied gently, "He was making a statement." But she didn't explain, and she went on upstairs and to her room where she closed her door.

*   *   *

After dinner on Sunday, there could be no real surprise when Tom sorta hurried them through the dish-clearing commitment and headed Susan Lee toward the front door. Tom actually listened for it. Her mother said, "Oh, I promised the boys you'd take them along to see the dog."

Even Tom understood that one. He surveyed the two, one eight and one twelve; then he glanced over at Susan Lee to check her out again. Her face and body hadn't deteriorated even the barest shade. She was still just like always. He'd endure anything to be with her. Whatever it would take. He said to the boys, "Wanna change your duds?"

They didn't even reply. They thundered off up the stairs and slammed doors. Susan Lee followed in a sedate, show-offy manner. The boys returned in an amazingly brief interval and went right out to Tom's car.

Tom escorted a jeans-clad Susan Lee to the car, told the boys to get in back and seated her on the passenger side of the front. He went around and got into the other side. On their way to the Petersons', he spent the entire time explaining to the boys the workings of the car and all the gadgets.

He got entangled in that. Once he stopped and raised the hood so the boys understood better.

At the Petersons', Tom changed into jeans. Then he selected two of the Petersons to go along, and that relieved him of the chore of being host. The boys were told a couple of times to "Cut that out!"

Tom stopped once and sorted the four out. They were laughing so hard that it wasn't easy. Then he

threatened the foursome, and they behaved...
enough.

The dog was there. The boys had to stay in the car.
Tom told them to be silent. They became more aware
when Susan was given the rifle, and they heard as she
took off the safety.

She told the boys, "There was something moving last
time up on that ridge. Keep your eyes open."

That made it more interesting.

Tom replenished the food and added a great bone
from the McCrea Sunday roast. He refilled the water
pan that had once been his car's hubcap; then he
backed off enough and waited as the dog decided he
could go and investigate the bone.

The dog did that.

In her soft voice, Susan Lee told the foursome to be
silent or she'd rip out their vocal cords.

They were silent. They knew about soft-speaking
women.

Tom talked to the dog, and the dog did listen. He
looked at Tom and he looked over at the car.

The older of Susan Lee's siblings said in a hushed
voice, "That dog needs a boy. He wants us to come out
of the car."

In a deadly soft tone, Susan Lee said, "I thought I
warned you—"

And the brother said, "Yes'um."

So the car was silent. The boys sat in a row, controlling their curiosity enough but watching avidly.

Tom went slowly over to the dog and stood close.
The dog didn't move. His attention was riveted as he
listened and watched Tom.

Tom moved around slowly and shifted and looked around. The dog was silent and still. He wasn't spooked by Tom's movements.

Finally Tom poured more water into the pan, and he came back to the car. The dog trailed along about half way.

One of the Petersons started to whistle and was stopped dead in his effort by one of Susan Lee's searing glances.

That was especially impressive since the Petersons had a very loose discipline that mostly consisted of Geo saying they were a nuisance.

Tom came around the car and slid into the driver's seat. They all sat and watched the dog, who stood looking at them. One of the boys whispered, "He wants to come along. Can I open the door?"

"May...you."

"May I?" His voice went up in delighted confidence.

Tom replied a very soft, life-threatening, "No."

And the back seat was again silent.

That was when Susan Lee decided she'd marry Tom. He'd know how to handle kids. He'd showed them the motor and been patient, but he could also be firm. She glanced over at him, and he knew she was looking at him so he glanced back. She smiled.

That's when he knew he had her.

All they had to do was kill time before her family realized it was inevitable and they adjusted to the fact that their eldest was going to leave the nest.

Tom gave her another look that excited her stomach. It also sobered her, and she was very quiet.

Tom started the car and eased it away. As they gained the road, Tom told the boys, "Look back. He's on the road."

That released the boys to move and talk, which they did at high volume. They were so excited.

Susan Lee got out of her seat belt, knelt on her seat and told the boys, "Move! I want to see!"

So the passengers ducked aside, and she saw the big dog on the edge of the road, watching after them.

The boys said, "Let's go back and see if he'll get in the car!"

Tom said, "There's no room."

"I'll sit on the console," the twelve-year-old McCrea volunteered.

"You all are too noisy," Tom declared. "Hush, now."

And their yelling did go down about twelve decibels.

After that, the two were rarely alone, except for aide days on Tuesdays and Thursdays. Tom got to fetch her home from the hospital, and the McCreas were clock-watchers.

Every time there was an outing, someone was foisted on them with such interestingly contrived reasoning that the pair couldn't doubt they were being child chaperoned. Tom had his camera, of course, and pictures were taken and sold to the families. The time with the hangers-on was monetarily worthwhile. Otherwise it was frustrating.

The irritating part was the hostile but satisfied look on Garth's face. Garth knew the pair was never alone, and he was sure time was on his side. Susan Lee would tire of Tom and come back to Garth Pippins, who was a solid man who had land.

It was amazing the errands that Susan Lee needed to run that required another person in Tom's car. Or there were people who needed a ride home. It was astounding that happened so frequently.

Even when Tom picked Susan Lee up at the hospital, it seemed there was always another aide who needed a last-minute ride. It was too often.

But Yankees are sly, everyone knows that, and even an eight-year Texas convert retains a sneaky Yankee trick or two.

They were overloaded with chaperons on one of their outings and took the McCrea batch home first, then they delivered the Peterson contingent and—what a surprise—there the pair was... all alone, just the two of them, together in the isolation of his car.

He smiled at her, and they both laughed. He said, "I have a place that you'll just love."

"What place?"

"You'll see."

He drove along with rather more dispatch than he'd been driving in those weeks. And they came to the barn that had been abandoned to nature for some long time. He pulled in past the barn into the lacy covering of the concealing mesquites.

He got out, but she was still in the car. He went around and said, "Come with me. I want to show you paradise."

"In that old barn?"

"We'll buy this land and put a dome over the barn. I want you so badly that I'm about to die."

"Here?"

"I promise, you won't notice."

And she laughed so softly and with such delightful humor that he was lost forever. He told her, "How do I love thee..."

And she replied, "Let me count the ways."

"Ahh, Susan Lee, you thrill my soul."

She did glance at that tacky barn. But the moon was a thin sliver so that all the billions and billions of TEXAS stars were like diamonds sparkling in the sky. The light they cast on the precious earth that belonged to TEXAS was as strikingly silvered as it was with moonlight. The barn was a miracle of stark light and shadow. Beautiful.

He said, "Starlight, starbright, I have my wish tonight."

"I'm a little shy."

"Don't be. We'll be doing this forever and ever, even after all this world is gone."

She looked around. "I'd hate for so precious a planet to be ruined or to disappear. Creatures should have it as it was, even if we don't survive as a people."

"It will." And he promised, "We will."

"How can you be sure?"

"It's so unique. It must. It is perfect. Like you. Aw, my love." And he held her to him and kissed her. His fuse was lit immediately. She was slower.

He told her, "This place has been ready since I walked you out to the parking lot that first time."

She was a little indignant. She asked rather formally, "You thought I was easy?"

"Well... I *did* think it would be easier to get you alone than it has been. Just lately, I've had to brush people off us like fire ants."

"Do you love me?"

"Haven't I told you that enough?"

"The various kids in the back seat must have out-shouted you."

"I love you. I'm going to marry you, and we're go-ing to live happily ever after. My brother Rod up in Indiana is living happily ever after. So are the others, but he is particularly. Our lives will go like his."

"How can you be so sure?"

"I know."

He held her close and kissed her so that her brain spun inside her head and her resistance melted. She gasped and pawed at him and made little hungry sounds.

He watched the starlight on her body as he took off her clothing, and he was overwhelmed and—almost—wanted his camera. She was shy with him, and even the starlight didn't hide the blushes that suffused her. But she wasn't at all hesitant. She helped him out of his clothes, and she was tidy in folding his. Hers were strewn around somewhat. She paid those no immedi-ate attention, she was too busy peeking at him.

He showed her the nest he'd contrived inside the barn. He gathered her clothes and put them on a slanting board with his. Then he stooped down and went inside. She followed.

There were thick blankets, pillows…and a barn cat.

The cat hissed at their intrusion.

Tom said, "Sorry, you can come back later. Scat for now."

The cat did so in a huffy manner. They were the in-truders.

Susan Lee expected Tom to be very sudden. She knew he'd been pitched for a long time, and she just braced for his hunger. She had read quite a good book on this very act, and she knew what to expect after the first fumbling, embarrassing time.

But Tom surprised her. He was so patient and slow with her that he was wonderful. He kissed her really sweetly and ran his hands over her, making admiring sounds and murmurs of appreciation.

The starlight through the ruins allowed them to see each other—enough. She was so self-conscious. How can a woman know what a man expects? She thought her breasts weren't very big, and he'd be disappointed.

His hands caressed them and admired them, and he kissed them. He murmured and rubbed his face on them, and he saluted the peaks with a hungry mouth. He curled her toes and shivered the insides of her thighs.

She slid glances at his body, and his sex surprised her. She'd seen her little brothers naked, but a man's sex was considerably different. She was another who wasn't sure it would work. It was too big. She tightened.

But he wasn't pushy. He lay beside her and rubbed his hand on her stomach and up over her breasts and down her side to her thighs.

He kissed her marvelously and stroked her perfectly. She began to heat.

She said, "You can go ahead."

He replied, "This isn't something to get past, this is something wonderful. Let's take it easy and enjoy the preliminaries."

"What should I do?"

"You could rub my stomach."

She did that. "It's hairy."

"I'll shave it."

"No! I like hairy stomachs."

"How do you know that?"

"I've seen hairy stomachs."

"When?" A very brief word for such a question. "You rubbed Garth's stomach?"

"Is his hairy? How do you know that?"

"I don't, but more interesting, neither do you."

"I've never rubbed any man's stomach. Do you like that?"

"Yeah. Go a little lower."

She giggled, "Why is it jumping around like that?"

"It's happy."

She laughed in her throat. "Does it want to be rubbed, too?"

"Oh...yesss." Then he added, hastily realistic, "But maybe not right away. Maybe you'd like to see how I'm made."

"I do have brothers. I saw them when they were little."

"Men are somewhat different." He mentioned that with a rather foggy voice.

"I see."

Her comment caught his attention. "What do you see?"

"That you're very different from a little boy."

His voice was still foggy, but it was very tender. "It'll fit."

"I was wondering."

"And it feels wonderful."

"Even the first time?"

"We'll go slow and be careful and not rush us."

"Oh, good." And she relaxed.

He made love to her. And she loved it. She murmured and said a whole lot of *mmm's* and she rubbed her knees together and encouraged him.

He was slow. His movements were slow, his hands, his mouth, he was amazingly slow...and he was patient.

She became less so. She pushed her chest against him for his attention, she opened her thighs to his hands, she lifted her mouth for another kiss...and she touched him gently.

He drew in his breath so sharply that she thought she'd hurt him. And she gasped a sympathetic sound and took her hand away quickly.

He urged, "Do it again." And he moved himself to be more available to her.

"Didn't that hurt?"

His deep voice was rusty, "Ohhh, nooo."

She laughed such a bubble of delight. Sobering, she watched as he coaxed his shaky hands to roll on the condom. And he hugged her bare, soft sweetness to his hard, hairy, ready body.

She said, "Mmm." The *m's* multiplied outrageously with his attentions. She was fortunate to have the opportunity to get rid of some more.

"You like that?" he'd ask.

And she could get rid of more of the *m's*. She sighed and moved languidly, and she rubbed her body against his invitingly.

He wondered if she knew how erotic that was for him. He held her as if she was precious.

She wiggled slowly and moved, slithering along him. She opened her mouth on his skin and licked along him.

He shivered and gasped and made hoarse sounds.

She looked up at him through her tumbled hair and asked, "Do you like that?"

"Wait a minute."

"I need to be sure your tummy button is clean."

"In just a minute."

She leaned over him and lowered her mouth, and his sex thumped against her breast. She raised up and said to it, "You'll have your turn, behave!"

And those words just about set him off. He said, "I have to go lift the car."

She raised up and looked out into the starlight. "Is it stuck? How could you know it was stuck?"

"I need to calm down, I'm about to compete with a Fourth of July sky burst."

"Really?"

"I'll be right back."

She wasn't sure what was happening. She was interested. However, he was interrupting her adventure.

After he had gone out of their nest, she heard a sound and glanced up. It was the cat, watching. She asked silkily, "Learning anything new?"

The cat was owl eyed. Susan Lee told it, "I know just how shocked you must be. I am—almost."

Tom came back to their nest and stooped down to come back inside. "Who're you talking to?"

"The cat."

"Don't get friendly. I can handle one big male dog, but a female cat could overwhelm us."

"Then you need to behave more discreetly. You are making this sexual adventure appear really marvelous to me, and that cat could be influenced to the point she'd seduce the first male that came along."

"I have never in my life realized I could influence a cat."

"One never knows the ramifications of conduct."

"Have you cooled?"

"Not particularly. What about you?"

"I can hold out a little longer or until you really want me."

"I believe you could do that now."

"Well, I would like to fool around just a little more."

And she was receptive. She curled down and put her hands up on his shoulders. "How do you plan to go about that... fooling-around part?"

"Well, I'd do this... How was that?"

More *m*'s.

"And this... Do you like that?"

A goodly number of *m*'s were dispersed.

He moved his hand down and parted her thighs in a caressing way. She cooperated. He moved his gently seeking fingers.

A lot more *m*'s.

His breathing changed and he kissed her more deeply and rubbed his chest on hers.

She groaned.

He began to breathe audibly.

His hands stiffened, and his movements were more positive, less hesitant. She wiggled and squirmed for more attention. He gave it. She made very erotic sounds, and her breathing changed.

He finally lifted his body to fit on hers and he slowly moved so that he slid into her. He hesitated, and she squirmed and wiggled and fought to get all of him.

He whooshed air and made harsh sounds and allowed her to take him into her as he slowly sank down and was still. He fought for control. He struggled to be slow.

And under him, she slithered and squirmed and held on to him and breathed sounds that lifted his hair off his head and stimulated his libido too much.

He said, "Honey—"

She said, "Wow."

He groaned, "Sweetheart—"

She demanded, "Move!"

He did.

It was a race of delight, movements of ecstasy, a cascade of thrills. It was wondrous. And they raced up that spiral of delight and flew off the vortex into exquisite oblivion. As they fell back through that disorienting vortex, she opened her eyes in amazement and looked right into those of the cat.

So she convulsed and laughed.

They lay spent. Their breaths labored. Their hands flopped. Their bodies were inert.

When he could, he asked, "You laughed?"

"Is that rude?"

"No. I just haven't ever heard of a woman laughing at a climax before this. You're strange."

"The cat was watching."

And he laughed.

Ten

The lovers lay sprawled, and talked in idle nonsense. Tom said to his love, "I did warn you that I was gonna get you."

Susan Lee's voice was amused, chiding. "I thought you meant after we were married."

"If I'd waited *that* long, I'd have been a gaunt shadow of my former self. After we were married, you'd have gone wild as you waited for me to be physically rehabilitated. It would have been so terrible for your frustration that you should be grateful I was thoughtful enough to save you that anguish."

She bubbled laughter.

"As it is, you've just about wrecked me."

She protested, "I was very careful of you. I did try not to tempt you."

He scoffed, "You breathed."

"Just breathing does it?"

"With you." His voice was reedy and earnest. He kissed her differently. It was so gentle and cherishing.

Her heart was touched. She said, "Oh, Tom—"

Gradually they talked of how they had reacted to one another at first sight. He told how the first sight of her had whammied him and that she wouldn't really look at him.

"I was not going to be another number in your black book."

"An innocent, recent TEXAN like me?"

Their laughter was smothered. They were so relaxed, so contented. Susan Lee turned onto her stomach, braced on her elbows and had all of Tom's attention. She'd had it all along, but now especially so.

Needlessly, she flirted. And he watched her, mesmerized, his face softened as he smiled at her, his gaze caressing her. His big hand smoothed her hair and his fingers played with the strands in awkward gentleness. He was not skilled in such casual intimacy.

With reluctance, she said, "I need to get home. We have taken a long time since we deposited the kids at the Petersons'."

"Yeah." But he didn't move. He lay lax and easy.

She rolled over on her back and stretched.

He had to rise to his elbow and watch that.

She put her fingers into his hair and pulled his face down to kiss him. She blushed, she was so bold. One thing led to another, and again they made love. It was gentle and delicious and different from the first riveted time.

Their movements were slower and more caressing, but their attentions were just exactly as intense. She heard nothing of what sounded beyond their bodies, but he listened and occasionally glanced around.

Their climax was wonderful, slow and throbbing, and they relaxed to smile at each other. It was loving of another kind.

Tom helped Susan Lee dress. Their movements were lethargic. He was so inept. Was it deliberate?

She chided, "You're a little careless with your hands."

He chuckled softly.

He pulled on his own clothing with some carelessness. He looked marvelous. He was like a dark, disreputable highwayman with blue eyes.

He put her into his car with such reluctance. He had to hold her and kiss her. He didn't want to be apart from her.

He finally closed her door with just pressure. And he had to look around the magic world that held such wonderment.

He got into the driver's seat and said, "Come home with me."

"That would cause a scandal. What would the Petersons say?"

"Geo would tell us we're a nuisance. And Mim would shift the baby to another shoulder to call our attention to what happens when a man and a woman are too friendly."

"That would be sobering."

He told her in a gruff voice, "You have to marry me now that you've stolen my virginity."

She was so rude as to chuff laughter.

He was shocked. "You scarlet woman! How can you laugh at the loss of my innocence."

She lay lax with her head on the back of the seat and watched him with sleepy eyes.

He kept turning his head to look at her. It was fortunate there was no traffic. He told her, "You're a siren."

"I have a shrill voice?"

"You're the kind that lures sailors onto the rocks."

"I'd never do that."

Then Tom turned his head quickly and looked back. He slowed and watched in the rearview mirror, then put his arm up over the seat and looked back through the rear window.

"What is it?"

"I'm not sure, but I think that was Garth's car back there."

"Why would Garth's car be there?"

"He could be parked with some other tasty bit, or he could be watching for me."

"You must be mistaken."

"Possibly." But Tom watched his rearview mirror and kept track of his back trail.

He got her home all right, but Susan Lee had some trouble getting away from Tom. He couldn't bring himself to let go of her. When he finally walked her up to the porch, he sat in the swing, and she couldn't make herself go inside and leave him there.

By then, her mother had gone back to bed, so when Tom finally did leave, Susan Lee slipped into the house and up the stairs to her room without being intercepted. She slept the sleep of a blissful woman.

The next morning, her father asked her, "What time did you get in last night." It was an opening statement, not a question.

"I didn't look at the clock. We saw Garth Pippins's car out parked. He going with anyone we know? I couldn't believe it. He isn't like that."

So her father inquired, "Tom that kind?"

And she replied, "'Course not."

But her mother watched as Susan Lee looked off out the window with a little smile on her lips, and as she wandered around the house, absently touching things to which she paid not one bit of attention. How she stretched luxuriously and moved her shoulders. And as she vapidly smiled and smiled.

That night her mother told her father. "They'll be getting married."

And he replied, "They'd better."

Tom took Susan Lee over to the Fuller place to meet Tweed's wife, Connie. The visitors didn't have to take any chaperons along because Janella McCrea couldn't think of a way to include any.

Sam was delighted to have company, and the cook, Jake, made them an exquisitely special meal. The lovers didn't notice, and Tweed had to remind them to compliment the cook. They did that.

They saw the porch built in the oak tree about a half block through the trees from the house. And Connie said they'd have a big dance there, come summer. "You'll have to promise to come."

They were out looking at the canyon when the storm clouds came up along the horizon. They could have gone home then, but Tom delayed and they were caught in the downpour.

As Tom had expected, they were drenched. Back at the ranch, their clothes had to be dried before they could leave. Therefore the bridge had the time to be washed away and trap them at Sam's for several days.

Connie loaned Susan Lee some clothes, and Tweed's fit Tom well enough. It was as they sorted through his clothes that Tweed asked if Tom could need some condoms?

"Now, Tweed, you are a scandal!" Tom laughed and slapped his brother's shoulder.

Tweed said, "A man never knows what a woman might do, and he should always take precautionary steps."

"I was told that at Salty's knee."

"So you came prepared?"

"Sure. We're gonna be married as soon as her folks realize their baby girl is old enough for such."

"She's a gem."

"Yeah. It kinda scares me."

"Why?"

"How could I be so lucky?"

"Tell her that, on occasion."

"I haven't dared, so far. I'm still trying to make her feel like she's the lucky one."

And Tweed laughed. "Oh, to be that young and secure again."

"I got a guy that's disputing my claim."

"Need any backup?"

"I'd whistle."

"See to it."

The unreliable phone lines were down, but those far-flung places had ham radios. They called in to the McCreas' with their location and the fact that they were stranded at Sam Fuller's with Tom's brother and his wife. The last information was for the nosy listeners. And Susan Lee had to regret not being able to be at the hospital for her stint.

The four young people, with Sam and Jake, had a good visit, which included stories, the history of the place and a tour of the—different—paintings that Sam's late wife had created long ago.

The guest rooms were upstairs, down another hall at the back of the house and just across the hall from one another. Tom hardly waited for the lights to go out before he was in Susan Lee's bed.

She expressed scandalized surprise. But she giggled and that rather blew her contrived indignation. He soon had her as naked as he, and he showed her how nice it was to make love in a bed.

She said she missed the cat.

In those several days, Susan Lee also found out what it was like to make love on a haystack in a barn with rain drumming on the roof. She came to realize there were vast variances in loving. She was awed by the nuances. She just hoped their lives would be long enough to experience all the varieties of love.

Susan Lee lay in the arms of her sleeping lover and knew Tom would never be cruel. She had too many examples of his gentleness, not only to her but to others.

Of course, she'd never seen him riled. How would he behave if he was really angered?

She went to sleep thinking of how patient he'd been with the lost dog, how firm and tolerant he'd been with their variety of chaperons and, beyond that, to all the charming things he'd done around and to her. She knew he was a gentle man. He was an adult of good logic and conduct.

When the bridge was shored up and the stranded ones could depart, they said their thanks and goodbyes to their hosts and drove away. They were silent for some time, then Susan Lee said quietly, "It will be hard to go to bed alone."

He stopped the car to groan in empathy as he held and kissed her.

When he delivered her back to her house, her mother gave Tom a weighing glance and said, "Your sister-in-law sounds like a nice woman. I remember when your brother found her."

"She had a tough time of it."

"How is she now?"

"She's a strong woman and she found a good man in Tweed."

Janella smiled. "You like Tweed."

Tom nodded as he added, "And Connie. They're good people. That Sam Fuller is a fine man."

Then Janella was the one to nod. "How come you didn't bring some of the rain back with you? It stopped ten miles north of here."

"Darn," Tom replied with a grin. "We didn't even think of it. Next time we'll be sure it's spread around better. They got a real gully washer north of here."

"We just got some of the runoff. The streambeds are full."

"I remember seeing that for the first time with my brother John at Covington's. No idea of any storm west of there, and the water pouring through the gullies. It was impressive."

"That's why we warn you Yankees."

"Ma'am, you do offend this eight-year TEXAN." He grinned at Susan Lee's mother.

Janella grinned back.

So in front of his future mother-in-law, Tom leaned over and kissed her daughter goodbye. He smiled at his love, and she pinkened charmingly.

He then told Janella, "I'll be back."

"That doesn't surprise me."

"We've got to see to the dog," Tom explained. "I just left Susan Lee here long enough to change."

"Brice went out and refilled the hubcap each day. He saw the dog only once. He was back in the brush."

Tom nodded, "That was neighborly of Mr. McCrea. Thank him kindly."

"I will."

Then Tom looked back at his love and told her gently, "I'll be back."

"I'll be ready."

Tom tipped his Stetson to Mrs. McCrea and went down off the porch to his car.

Mrs. McCrea asked her daughter, "Did he behave?"

"Perfectly." Susan Lee went on into the house, and Mrs. McCrea was left on the porch to consider that reply.

When Tom returned, only Susan Lee came to the door. They went off by themselves, and they were so surprised that they didn't comment on the lack of chaperons until they were almost to the place where the dog had been.

Tom said, "Do you realize we're alone?"

"Scary, isn't it."

Tom grinned. "Is she burdening us with her trust or has she given up on us?"

"I won't ask."

That made Tom laugh as he reached over and waggled her head. She took his hand and kissed it. He told her not to flirt yet.

Tom eased the car off the road and stopped. They looked over into the brush, and the dog was coming down from the ridge, looking around, but mostly at the car. He recognized the car?

Mostly just from habit, Tom gave the rifle to Susan Lee and got out of the car. He looked around. The dog was very alert. Its movements were different.

He said to Susan Lee, "The dog's jumpy. The cougar might be back. I'll be quick."

"Be careful."

"I most certainly will do so, my love. I'm not about to risk having to leave you here on this earth without me."

Tom moved in the pattern that allowed Susan Lee a clear shot at anything that might threaten him. The dog came and stood by the water pan. Tom approached and began to pour the water into the pan as he spoke to the dog.

The dog's attention was beyond and intense. Tom considered the cougar must be around and that consideration almost prepared him for what happened.

The boar erupted from the brush in a snorting, squealing charge!

Tom was shocked.

The yellow dog moved to counter and began to bark very seriously, but the boar was making a beeline for Tom!

The dog ran alongside the boar, nipping at the boar, snarling and vicious! He shouldered into the boar! The boar was temporarily distracted and squealed, grunting.

Tom ran full out for the car as Susan Lee fired the rifle. The bedlam of dog and rifle shots under the alarming, snorting squeals of the boar was shocking.

Susan couldn't stop firing to open the back door or put the key into the damned ignition to turn it on to work the damned windows.

Tom leapt up onto the hood and, from there, over onto the roof of the car. The boar was too close behind and savagely leapt unsuccessfully after the man who was then out of reach.

The dog snarled, backed and feinted, hampering the boar, which turned in fiery temper to the dog. The dog had to run across the highway, full out, to escape!

The boar snorted squeals and followed furiously just as the postman's car came along. The watching pair from Tom's car were riveted as the car missed the dog with screeching brakes and a blinding swirl of dust, which obliterated their vision.

But the car hit the boar. Tom jumped down from his car's hood, took the rifle from Susan Lee and shot the thrashing boar.

The postman, Mr. Tiller, got out of his car and said, "What the h— My God, man, are you all right?"

The dog was back, exuberantly calm. A partner in the melee. He pranced around, checked everyone out and barked at the prone, blood-oozing boar, which was still kicking in its death throes.

Mr. Tiller scrambled back to his opened car door cautiously and questioned, "Is it really dead? Where in hell did that come from? Is that you, Tom? Where'd you get that dog?"

Tom said, "Be careful. They're hard to kill." He told the dog, "Heel!"

The dog came to him, and Tom put his hand on the dog's head. It was the first time he'd touched the dog. The dog was full of himself and glad to share the excitement.

Tom said softly to the dog, "So that was why you were so pitched when we got here. You'd seen the boar."

The dog barked once as if in reply.

Tom went to the downed boar and put a bullet through its head. There was nothing more difficult to kill than a wild pig or boar. Seemingly dead and full of bullets, they could rise up and attack. No knowledgeable hunter took a boar's death for granted.

Mr. Tiller came cautiously from his car. "Is it dead?"

"How can you tell with a boar?"

"Yeah. I've heard that. Where'd it come from?"

Tom said quite seriously, "That is a question."

"I heard there was some, twenty miles east, down yonder in that old gully on the Butlers' place, the other side of their seep. I'd never heard of none around here."

And Tom replied softly, "Neither had I."

"Wonder if he fell off a truck?" Tiller asked. "How'd he get here?"

"I don't know."

"Be careful," Tiller cautioned. "He could have some sows around."

"Yes. Susan Lee, stay in the car."

Mr. Tiller asked, "That your dog? He's a beauty. I hadn't heard Geo had such a dog."

"He isn't Geo's," Tom replied. "He was probably lost. He'd gone wild. I've been giving him water for some time."

"Good thing for you," Tiller commented earnestly. "Without him around, you'd'a been mincemeat."

Even more softly, Tom said, "Yeah." Then Tom told Susan Lee, "I have to see if there're any more around. Stay in the car."

Mr. Tiller said, "I'll help. Let me get my gun. I need to get my car off the road."

"I'll drag the boar off."

"I'll help you. It's a big 'un."

They did all that and went into the brush.

Susan Lee found she was furious with Tom for going to look. He should have found some men with dogs to help. That area was part of the Fuquay place. They'd be delighted to help. Why hadn't Tom waited? What an irritating man!

And the fact that she had gone from mush, to shock, to terror, to relief, to anger did give her pause. She had never considered that she could be this furious with Tom's conduct. This hunter facade was something new. He'd appeared to be fairly civilized up until then.

She sat there in the car with the windows almost closed, rapidly getting a really impressive tension headache.

The two men and the prancing, interested, alert dog returned. Tom had brought back his hubcap, and he squatted down and put it back on the waiting wheel with some obvious satisfaction.

Tom opened the back door and on command, the dog got into the back seat and lay down obediently, without hesitation. He and Tom had—bonded?

Tom opened up the car trunk. He and Mr. Tiller heaved the carcass of the boar into the trunk, onto a tarpaulin Tom had opened out.

Tom went with Mr. Tiller to inspect the front of Tiller's car for damage from hitting the boar. They talked for a couple of minutes. Tom shook hands with Mr. Tiller and waved him off.

Then Tom came around the car, slid the gun along the side of his seat and got into the driver's seat. He asked, "Are you okay?"

She looked at him coldly.

He appeared not to notice her hostility, but busily buckled his seat belt as he said, "You're the best backup I've ever had. Thank you. Can you believe the dog is in the back seat right behind us and not trying to scratch his way out of the car?"

Probably the most irritating thing about a man is that he can lure a woman into conversation when she isn't speaking to him. She said, "I can't believe any of this happened."

"When I realize it did, I'll probably get a serious case of the shakes."

She confessed, with some bravery, "I thought I was going to have to get out of the car and go save you."

He instantly stopped what he was doing and gave her a very serious look. "If you'd gotten out of the car, I would have died of heart failure. If I ask you to stay someplace, do it."

She looked at him with some hostility. She was her own woman. She controlled her own life.

He leaned over and put his hand along her face. "Are you okay?"

"Of course."

He smiled so sweetly. "If the damned mesquites were taller, I wouldn't have had to get on top of the car. I was scared to death the damned boar might try to get through your window. How could you have closed it with the motor off?"

"I'd have put the gun down its throat and pulled the trigger."

"Wow."

They drove back to the Petersons' to get rid of the boar, and it was then that the lost dog was introduced to the Peterson dogs.

The lost one was a gentleman. He stood still and listened to the challenges. He allowed the bunch to sniff him and sniffed in turn. They no longer barked. The tails wagged, and the dogs relaxed.

Geo knew exactly what to do about the boar. He slit it and hung it and bled it. The kettles were filled with water and set and fires were started. Mim called all the neighbors to come over for the cracklings and for a picnic and for meat to take home to their freezers.

The McCreas were included, since they would soon be a part of Tom's family.

And the Pippinses were invited.

Even with the dogs' tolerance of him, the lost one was aloof. He stayed by Tom and watched everyone. Oddly enough, he watched Garth.

Garth held out a hand to the dog, but the dog shied away from him. Billy said, "You see that? Dogs like Garth."

Geo heard that.

And it was Billy Pippins who said, "The car hitting the boar and him scraping along the road almost hides it, but doesn't that look like the boar fought a rope recently? Do you suppose somebody was foolish enough to try to hog-tie him?"

Then Harry Clayburn said, "You know, that boar's ear is just like the one that was causing all the trouble down our way."

Mr. Pippins bent over and turned his head upside down so that he could look at it better and said, "That sure looks similar."

The men stood around talking, speculating, having a beer, while the women did the cooking and set the tables outside. And the men asked Tom, "He your dog?"

"I don't know."

And another said, "I'd be glad to take him off your hands."

Tom replied, "I'll have to ask the vet if such a dog is missing anywhere around. If he isn't claimed, I'd like to keep him."

"What'd you name him?"

"Nothing until I find out if he can stay. Then I think...I'd...name him...Hunter."

They all agreed that'd be a good name.

It was a long afternoon. They had good visiting, and the boar was butchered. The cracklings were cooked and fished out and relished. The younger kids all played, and the older ones stood around and talked and laughed and were separate from the kids and the adults.

It was getting toward evening. They'd eaten and some were lounged around, while the others cleared things away. The talk turned to whether the boar they'd just sampled was the same boar that had been down past the Clayburn place.

There was a niggling suspicion that was so, and it made an interesting subject to the people who were so familiar that new subjects didn't often show up.

If this was the same boar, why had it suddenly turned up that distance away?

It was Geo who suggested some of them go see if they could find any evidence that the porkers had migrated.

Clayburn said the sows were still around his place. He couldn't imagine why the boar would leave them there and just take off. Especially at that time.

Geo was the one who organized the search. He gathered a few men. Most of the others were willing to wait another day or two. Those who would stay behind chuffed at Geo organizing a project when they were all so full of food and contentment.

But that was Geo. He got a bee in his bonnet and whatever it was that moved him, was done.

Geo had seen to it that the Pippinses were along. He had tapped Clayburn, of course, and Tom, but he had included Brice McCrea.

Billy Pippins was enthusiastic and took the wheel of their Jeep. A silent Garth rode with him. Mr. Pippins was with Brice and Geo. The others were in other vehicles.

They found the evidence almost right away. It was as if Geo knew where to look. It was almost a beeline from the Pippins place to where the dog had been. The boar had been dragged a good deal of the time. It had fought the rope. The jeep had gone slowly.

There was one back tire mark that left a clear but slightly altered tread. It was nothing for Geo to check the treads of the stopped vehicles. And they all saw that the tread was that of the Pippinses' Jeep.

Garth was mute. Billy was shocked.

Tom stood up silently and his body came from the slouch into a very dangerous stance. Susan Lee had been put in jeopardy. Geo took Tom's arm in his hand and said, "Leave it."

No one made any other comment. Most of them re-turned to the Petersons' place where Mr. Pippins told Tom, "I'm sorry for this."

And Tom replied, "I understand."

The next day, Garth Pippins went to some relatives off in California. The Pippins family were apologetic. But they were honest. They told Tom, "Look at her. You of all people ought to understand Garth."

And Tom did understand.

In the years that followed, he would look at his wife and shiver a little as he considered what it would have been like to have lost her to any other man. She was his. He would ask her. "Do you realize you belong to me?"

And she would reply, "I chose you."

Almost all of the widely flung Browns went to Tom's marriage to Susan Lee McCrea. It was a gala. There were so many people there that they took the idea from Tweed's wedding and put up tents. They were in a field of bluebonnets and Indian paintbrushes, the cart-wheels and all the marvels of the Texas spring flowers.

Susan Lee was so beautiful a bride that she put all those beautiful flowers to shame.

No one claimed the dog. He was such a superb ani-mal that on occasion Tom felt sorrow for the man who'd lost him. While the dog lived with them, Tom called him Hunter.

Tom settled in that area. In the years that followed, he still was the camera artist, but he did love taking pictures of people. His camera made people look as they thought they did, but instead of plastic beauty, they were the people who were in their souls.

Susan Lee got her doctorate, and did her thesis on male behavior, but it wasn't the snide and sly one she'd threatened to write.

They had a good life among good people. And the TEXICAN-adopted Brown families proliferated and were a good bunch.

* * * * *

SILHOUETTE® Desire®

Coming in May
from Silhouette Desire

When an

Irresistible!

man meets an unattainable woman...
sparks fly!

Look for these exciting men in books
created by some of the top authors in
contemporary romance:

#853   LUCY AND THE STONE by Dixie Browning
        (Man of the Month)
#854   PERSISTENT LADY by Jackie Merritt
#855   BOTHERED by Jennifer Greene
#856   A LAWLESS MAN by Elizabeth Bevarly
#857   ONCE UPON A FULL MOON by Helen R. Myers
#858   WISH UPON A STARR by Nancy Martin

Don't miss them—only from Silhouette Desire!

SILHOUETTE®

Desire®

**Coming Next Month
from Silhouette Desire**

THE BRAINY BEAUTY
Suzanne Simms

**The first book in her
delightful new series**

HAZARDS INC.

Meet the Hazard men: Jonathan, Nick, Simon and
Mathis. Together they run Hazards Inc., a top-notch
security operation. But if danger is their business...
love is their reward!

Look for *The Brainy Beauty* (SD #850) in April and
The Pirate Princess (SD #862) in June. And Hazards, Inc.
will continue in 1995 with two more delectable love
stories—only from *Silhouette Desire!*

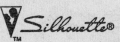